MYSTERY AT DEVIL'S PAW

When Frank and Joe Hardy receive a telegram from Tony Prito in Alaska telling them that his life is in jeopardy, they immediately make plans to fly to Tony's rescue.

Unknown enemies dog the Hardys and their pal Chet Morton even before they start the 4,000-mile journey. The forces working against them become increasingly menacing in Juneau, where Frank and Joe nearly lose their lives. Who are the vicious assailants? And what are their sinister motives? Trying to find the answers to these puzzling questions lead the Hardys into dangerous sleuthing in the wilderness of Alaska and British Columbia.

The astounding secret that the young detectives uncover, in the shadow of the forbidding mountain peak Devil's Paw, winds up one of the most perilous adventures they have ever encountered.

"Look out below!" Joe cried.

Hardy Boys Mystery Stories

MYSTERY AT DEVIL'S PAW

BY

FRANKLIN W. DIXON

NEW YORK
GROSSET & DUNLAP
A NATIONAL GENERAL COMPANY
Publishers

Printed in the United States of America

CONTENTS

MYSTERY AT
DEVIL'S PAW

CHAPTER I

Highway Attack

"TELEGRAM for Frank and Joe Hardy!"

The messenger gave an envelope to the seventeen-year-old, blond-haired boy who answered the door at the Hardys' home in Bayport. Joe signed for it and hurried into the living room.

"Who's it from?" Frank Hardy asked excitedly. The dark-haired boy, a year older than Joe, waited patiently while his brother slit the envelope and took out the telegram.

"It's from Tony!" Joe exclaimed. "And it sounds urgent!" He read:

BELIEVE I HAVE STUMBLED ON A WEIRD MYS-
TERY. MY LIFE MAY BE IN DANGER. TRY TO
COME RIGHT AWAY AND BRING CHET MORTON.
WHEN YOU ARRIVE JUNEAU ASK FOR TED SEW-
ELL AT SEAPLANE BASE.

Tony Prito, a good friend of the Hardy boys,

1

had gone to Alaska the week before to take a summer job as stream guard with the Fish and Wildlife Service.

"He must be in real trouble," Frank said, frowning. "I'm sure Mom and Dad will let us go."

Fenton Hardy, the boys' father, had been a famous detective in the New York City Police Department. After he left the force and moved to Bayport, the tall, athletic-looking sleuth had gained even more renown when he became a private investigator. Frank and Joe, who had inherited their father's zeal for bringing criminals to justice, often helped him unravel his complicated cases and had solved several mysteries completely on their own.

The two boys hurried out to the garden in back of the house, where Mr. and Mrs. Hardy were seated on lawn chairs, enjoying the afternoon sunshine. Gertrude Hardy, the boys' tall, thin aunt, was serving glasses of iced tea.

"Dad!" Joe cried excitedly. "May Frank and I go to Alaska?"

"Just like that?" Fenton Hardy chuckled. "Sit down and tell us what this is all about."

"Humph!" put in Aunt Gertrude. "Sounds like another mystery to me. I can always tell the symptoms! You'll freeze to death in Alaska. Mark my words!"

"Oh, Aunty," Joe said. "Alaska isn't all ice and

snow. A few days ago it was eighty degrees in Juneau."

"Seems incredible," Mr. Hardy agreed, "but it's true. The Alaskan Panhandle has weather much like Washington or Oregon, with plenty of rain."

"Then you'll both get wet and die of pneumonia!" Aunt Gertrude went on.

The boys suppressed a smile as the conversation about the state continued. Only the far north was frigid, Joe recalled from his social studies. He knew that Alaska was an Aleut Indian name meaning "Great Land."

"We can't leave Tony stranded," Frank pleaded. He showed his father the telegram.

Fenton Hardy scanned the message, reflected a moment, then passed it to his wife. "What do you think, Laura?"

Mrs. Hardy, a slim, pretty woman, read the telegram with a slight frown. "It sounds rather dangerous."

"Of course it's dangerous!" Aunt Gertrude read the telegram over Mrs. Hardy's shoulder. "Alaska is full of man-killing bears and treacherous glaciers," she warned. "And besides, I heard a rumor on a newscast last week. A United States rocket was programmed to crash-land in the White Sands Missile Range near El Paso after going up 400,000 feet. Instead, it misfired and dropped in Alaska."

"But what's that got to do with our helping Tony?" Frank asked.

"It could happen again!" Miss Hardy retorted in a peppery tone.

"Boy, that would make our trip even more exciting!" Joe said, his eyes twinkling mischievously.

Aunt Gertrude sighed deeply. "Won't you boys ever take my advice?" she fumed.

After a moment's thought, Mrs. Hardy said, "I'll leave the decision to your father."

The detective smiled as Frank asked eagerly, "Could we take your plane, Dad?"

Under the direction of Jack Wayne, Mr. Hardy's pilot, both Frank and Joe had become experts at piloting their father's six-place, single-engine craft.

"I'm afraid not, son," Mr. Hardy replied. "I need it myself. Jack is flying me to Miami to wind up an investigation." Mr. Hardy looked at his sons quizzically. "It will cost quite a bit to fly to Alaska on the regular airlines."

"We've thought of that, Dad," Frank said. "Joe and I have saved several hundred dollars from odd jobs. We were putting it aside for an outboard motor."

"But Tony comes first!" Joe added stoutly.

The detective was impressed by his sons' loyalty to their friend, and said so. "All right, you have the go-ahead from me, boys. I'll chip in a few more dollars if you need it!"

"Great, Dad!" Frank pumped his father's hand, while Joe, seized with enthusiasm, waltzed his mother around until she protested that she was getting dizzy.

Jubilant, the boys telephoned Chet Morton. Chet, a stocky, good-natured boy, was the Hardys' friend and classmate at Bayport High.

"I'll ask my folks if I can go along, too," their pal replied after hearing the news.

"Well, make it snappy," Frank urged. "We'll have to get plane reservations right away."

Chet promised to let them know his parents' decision as soon as possible and hung up.

Twenty minutes later his noisy jalopy chugged up in front of the Hardys' pleasant, tree-shaded home. The boys ran out to greet him.

"Can you come on the trip?" Frank asked.

Chet looked worried. "It's okay with my folks, but—well, I'm not sure I ought to go."

"Why not?" Joe demanded. "If Tony's in trouble, you want to help him, don't you?"

"Yes," but that's just it—the *danger*," Chet replied nervously. "How do I know we won't get plugged by gold thieves or someone? Last time I took a trip with you fellows, I got tossed in an underground dungeon!"

Chet was referring to their recent adventure in

Puerto Rico, where the Hardy boys had tracked down an international ring of lawbreakers in a case called *The Ghost at Skeleton Rock*.

"Stop worrying." Frank chuckled. "Think of the salmon fishing in Alaska! Can't you visualize a nice plump Chinook salmon sizzling on the fire?"

"Mm, boy!" Chet immediately perked up. "Well, okay. We can't let Tony down!"

"That's the spirit," said Joe. "Let's phone for plane reservations!"

The three hurried inside and stood by while Frank dialed the airport ticket office. "Line's busy," he announced impatiently.

After trying for several minutes without success to contact the airport, the Hardys decided to drive there.

"We can take my jalopy," Chet said. "It'll get us out there in a jiffy!"

"In one piece?" Frank asked, winking at Joe.

"Hop aboard!" Chet commanded.

When the trio had squeezed in, he threw the car into gear and started off with a roar.

Soon they were rolling along the highway toward the airport. When they reached the flight terminal, Frank asked the clerk at the ticket counter for three reservations to Juneau, Alaska.

"How soon do you want to leave?" the clerk inquired.

"Tomorrow morning."

The clerk shook his head. "Sorry, but we're booked solid for the next two days as far as Chicago. That's where you'll make flight connections."

The boys looked at each other in dismay.

"Will you put us on your list for tomorrow's flight in case there are any cancellations?" Frank asked.

"Certainly. But you'll have to be standing by at flight time. Of course I can't guarantee accommodations."

Frank nodded and gave their names and addresses. Then the boys turned to leave.

"If we can't get space in the next twenty-four hours, let's hop a train or bus," Joe suggested.

Frank and Chet both agreed to this. As they walked away from the counter, Joe gave his brother a slight nudge.

"What's up?" Frank asked quietly.

"Take a look at that man next to the water cooler. He's been listening to everything we said."

The stranger, dark-haired and with piercing eyes, seemed to realize that the boys were talking about him. Hastily he walked away and strode out the front door of the terminal.

"Who is he?" asked Chet.

"Search me," Joe replied. "Maybe he was just nosy, but he might have had a reason for eavesdropping on us."

They hurried out of the building and looked

around, but the man had disappeared. The trio climbed into the jalopy and headed back toward Bayport, with Chet clinging to the wheel like a racing driver.

"Give it more gas or we'll be arrested for holding up traffic," Joe teased.

Glancing at his rear-view mirror, Chet remarked, "That truck in back of us certainly is highballing."

Frank and Joe turned to look. The driver of a large black vehicle was far exceeding the speed limit.

"Give that cowboy plenty of room to pass," Frank said.

"Right." Chet drove closer to the side of the road, only inches from the edge of a ditch which separated the highway from a strip of wooded land.

As the truck drew up behind him, he gave the signal to pass. Suddenly he looked to his left and exclaimed, "Hey, stop crowding me!"

"Look out there!" Joe cried. The truck's cab was so high that he could not see the driver.

The next instant the side of the truck brushed Chet's jalopy. With a sickening scraping sound and the shriek of rubber against pavement, the boy's car tumbled into the ditch, coming to rest on its side. Seconds later, dazed from the accident, the Hardys crawled clear of the jalopy. The truck was out of sight.

Chet's car tumbled into the ditch!

"Oh, oh, my head," Joe groaned as he struggled to collect his wits. Chet was stunned and did not move.

The Hardys eased their friend gently from the car. While they were trying to revive him, several passing motorists stopped to offer assistance.

"I'll call the police," a woman promised. "There's a gas station not far from here."

In a matter of minutes, a State Police car arrived at the scene and two officers got out. Chet was just regaining consciousness.

"Need an ambulance?" one of the troopers asked.

"N-no, I'm okay," Chet said woozily. "But I sure feel sore all over!"

Frank and Joe reported the accident to the officers. "That guy must have a grudge against us. He deliberately forced us into the ditch!" Joe said hotly.

"It's possible," one of the troopers commented. "Did you have a chance to get his license number?"

"No, sir. It all happened too fast," Frank replied glumly, but he gave a complete description of the vehicle.

The troopers made a sketch of the scene of the accident and talked to several of the witnesses, writing down their names and addresses. When they had all the information they needed, one of them said to Chet, "A wrecker will be here soon to tow your car in for repairs." He wrote down the name of the garage and handed it to Chet.

"Meanwhile," he went on, "we'd better take you to a hospital."

Even though the boys protested that they felt fine, the officers dropped them off at Bayport Hospital, where a doctor examined them. After bandaging a cut on Chet's head, he suggested that the Hardys' friend rest in bed until fully recovered.

Frank and Joe, miraculously, had only minor bruises.

Chet was driven to the Morton farm. Then Frank and Joe accompanied the officers to Bayport Police Headquarters. After hearing their story, Chief Collig, an old friend of the Hardys, asked:

"Any idea who might be responsible?"

Frank shook his head. "Not unless someone is trying to keep us from going to Alaska." He explained about Tony Prito's telegram and the eavesdropper at the airport.

"Well," said Chief Collig, "our prowl cars and the State Police will keep looking for that truck."

When they arrived home, the Hardys told their father what had happened. Mr. Hardy looked grave. "I'm afraid this proves that you're up against a nasty enemy," he commented. "Better not mention the attack to your mother or Aunt Gertrude."

Frank and Joe went to bed that night sobered by the thought that they were tackling a dangerous case. And what about Tony? Was he still safe or had he, too, met with some kind of "accident"?

The next morning Frank and Joe were heartened by a telephone call from Chet Morton, who said that he had recovered completely and would meet them at the airport.

After eating breakfast and packing their clothes, the boys said good-by to their family and drove off in their convertible.

"If we get on the plane," Frank said, "we'll leave the car in the parking lot until our return."

While taking their luggage out of the trunk, they saw Chet pull into the lot. Apparently his jalopy, though scratched and dented, was still roadworthy. Beside him sat two pretty girls.

"Hey! Iola and Callie!" Joe shouted.

"We came to see you off," said Chet's dark-haired sister, Iola Morton.

"I was hoping you might," Joe admitted with a grin.

"Ditto!" Frank said, smiling at his own favorite date, Callie Shaw.

"Don't get lost in that Alaskan wilderness," warned Callie, an attractive blonde with sparkling brown eyes.

"We'll try not to. Sure you're feeling okay, Chet?"

"Fit as a fiddle!"

The boys checked in at the ticket counter, then said good-by to the girls who left in Chet's car to keep a tennis date.

At ten o'clock the boys lined up at the outside gate as the Chicago-bound plane landed and taxied up to the airport building.

"Hey, look!" Joe whispered to his companions. "There's that man again!"

The stranger who had eavesdropped the day before was pacing nervously up and down, apparently unaware of the Hardys. As he strode past, Frank pointed to his footprint on a piece of paper lying on the ground. The heelmark showed a circle with a star in it.

Moments later, the loading ramp was wheeled up to the big airliner and the passengers streamed aboard. A voice over the public-address system began paging the Hardys, so the boys hurried back to check at the ticket counter.

"Two empty seats," the airline clerk told them.

The Hardys and Chet stared at one another in a quandary. If they accepted the seats, one of the trio would have to be left behind.

As they pondered, the suspicious stranger rushed angrily to the counter. "Now wait a minute!" he challenged. "Those seats were paid for by friends of mine. You have no right to assign them to someone else!"

"Oh, yes, we do," the clerk retorted. "If your

friends aren't on hand for the flight, they can ask for refunds later." Turning back to the boys, he added, "How about it?"

"B-b-but there's three of us!" Chet stuttered.

"You'll have to make up your minds," the clerk said. "I can't wait any longer."

CHAPTER II

Decoy

WHILE the stranger stood by, sulking, Frank said, "Look, there are other ways to get to Chicago."

"Sure," Chet agreed. "We can take a train."

"Okay," Joe said. "Let's go back to town."

As they left, Chet kept an eye on the man, who followed them closely.

"That creep's tailing us," he warned the Hardys.

"He's up to no good," Joe said. "I'd like to clobber him."

"Easy," Frank advised. "We can snare the snoop another way."

"What do you have in mind?" Chet asked.

The trio stopped to confer, while the stranger lolled against a phone booth trying to look nonchalant.

Joe pulled his wallet from his pocket and all

three boys pretended to examine some papers. They talked in low voices and nodded as if in full agreement about what was being said. The man intently watched their reflection in the glass door of the phone booth.

Joe moved as if to return the wallet to his pocket. But instead it fell to the concrete floor, apparently unobserved by the boys.

As the Hardys and Chet hastened out one of the doors, the man picked up the wallet. He looked about to see if anyone had noticed. But the passers-by paid no attention.

The man opened the wallet and took out the papers. But he did not have a chance to read them, because Joe came racing back. The fellow took off like a flash.

"Stop, thief!" Joe cried out. He ran after the man, followed closely by Frank and Chet.

Frank yelled, "Get him!"

People in the terminal craned their necks to see what was happening.

As the fugitive passed the Bayport Airways counter, Joe caught up to him. He tripped him neatly from behind and sent him sprawling. The stranger hit the polished terrazzo floor and slid along for a few feet, coming to a halt near a policeman who had rushed to the scene.

Frank and Joe collared the man and pulled him to his feet. He still held the wallet in his hand.

"That belongs to me!" Joe said.

The officer relieved the fugitive of the wallet. "What's going on here?" he asked.

Out of breath and stunned by his belly landing, the man said:

"I don't know who this belongs to. I found the wallet on the floor and wanted to take it to Lost and Found. These kids ran me down!"

The policeman opened the wallet and Joe readily identified it as his.

"Here, take it," the patrolman said. Then his eyes narrowed as he looked at the man. "Who are you? What's your name?"

"Henry Smith," the man replied.

"Well," the officer said, "next time you find a wallet—the Lost and Found office is in the other direction." He pointed to the far end of the terminal building.

Before the Hardys had time to quiz the stranger further, their names came booming over the loud-speaker.

"Will Frank and Joe Hardy and Chet Morton please report for standby seats!"

After a quick thank-you to the policeman, the boys left.

"I wonder what happened," Frank said as they walked to the ticket counter.

"You fellows are pretty lucky," said the clerk. He explained that a passenger had become sick and was being taken off the plane. "Now there are three seats available. Do you still want them?"

"Sure," Joe said. They hastily paid for the tickets and ran out to the airplane just as the jet motors whined into life.

"That was a piece of luck," Chet said as they took their seats.

Frank nodded. "But I still wish we could have interrogated Mr. Snoop."

"Well, he won't bother us for a while," Joe said.

The first leg of their trip proved uneventful. They landed in Chicago, and after a twenty-five-minute wait, boarded the Seattle flight. All three napped as they winged across the prairie states and the Rocky Mountains.

It was brisk and cool when they landed at Seattle-Tacoma airport. Frank, Joe, and Chet strolled into the passengers' lounge.

Glancing at the wall clock, Joe remarked, "An hour to go before we board the plane for Juneau."

"Look," Frank put in, "I think we should call Dad and tell him what happened back at Bayport just before we took off. He might be able to check on that man."

A row of telephone booths lined one wall of the waiting room. Frank stepped into a booth and put through a long-distance call to the Hardy home. Much to his amazement, his father knew all about the Bayport episode.

"I drove out to the airport to see if you boys had taken off yet," Mr. Hardy explained. "I reached the outside gate just as you were embarking. The guard, Dick Harper, is a friend of mine. He told me about the man who grabbed Joe's wallet. He was still there waiting for a passenger. A plane came in from the coast and he kept looking at the arrivals. Obviously the passenger he was to meet did not show, so he left. Anyhow, he looked familiar, so I played a hunch and followed him."

"Did you find out who he was?" Frank asked eagerly.

"Yes. He's a wanted spy named Romo Stransky," the detective replied. "I had him arrested and was hoping he'd talk, but he didn't."

"Too bad."

"You boys might be in real danger. Be careful."

"We'll watch out, Dad," Frank promised.

After hanging up, he stepped out of the booth. Joe was waiting outside. Chet, who had wandered away, came running toward them with a wild-eyed look.

"Hey, fellows, guess what! The guy we saw in Bayport this morning is here at the airport!"

"That's impossible, Chet," Frank declared. "Dad had him arrested!" Hastily he reported his telephone conversation with Mr. Hardy.

"Then Stransky must have a double," Chet insisted.

"Where did you spot him?" Frank asked.

"Right over there by the magazine stand." As Chet turned to point, his eyes widened in surprise. "He's gone!"

"Maybe we can still find him!" Joe urged.

The three boys made a fast circuit of the building. They also checked the parking lot and the outside gates that led to the flight apron. But Stransky's double was nowhere in sight.

"What a way to start this trip!" Chet wailed. "Here I was just going along for some nice salmon fishing. Now you've got me all mixed up with a bunch of spies and even seeing double!"

"Cheer up," Joe said. "You leave the spies to us, and we'll still get in some fishing."

Within an hour, a voice boomed out over the loudspeaker, "Flight for Juneau, Alaska, now loading at Gate Ten!"

The three boys trooped aboard and fastened their seat belts. Minutes later they were soaring high above the Pacific coast.

After winging over Vancouver Island, the jet flew steadily northward up the rugged Canadian coast. Majestic green-clad mountains towered up to snowy peaks, and the blue waters offshore were dotted with rocky islands.

"Boy, what vacation country!" Frank said enthusiastically.

Even Chet was relaxed now. "I'm sure glad that Tony sent for us," he said, beaming.

Favorable tail winds speeded their trip, and in

a few hours the boys sighted Juneau. The city lay nestled at the foot of a steep mountain.

"Where do we land?" Chet wondered aloud.

His question was answered a few minutes later as the plane came down on an airfield several miles to the north. From there, they were whisked by car back to Juneau along the beautiful Glacier Highway. Frank and Joe watched, but noticed no one trailing them. Soon the forested slopes of the mountain gave way to the outskirts of town.

"Jeepers, it's a real city," Chet remarked, eyeing the modern buildings.

"What did you expect—log cabins?" Joe chuckled. "Juneau is the capital of Alaska."

Chet whistled in amazement as they entered the attractive lobby of their hotel.

"I sure never expected anything like this!"

As soon as the bellhop had taken them to their rooms, Chet sank down on his comfortable bed. "Think I'll catch forty winks," he yawned. "That meal on the plane made me sleepy."

The Hardys grinned. "Okay," Joe said. "Frank and I will look up Ted Sewell."

Chet's heavy breathing indicated that he had drifted off to sleep even before the Hardys had unpacked their luggage.

"Well, Chet's in good country for sawing logs," Frank quipped as they slipped on sweaters and left the room.

At the desk in the lobby Joe asked directions

to the seaplane base. It was a five-minute walk. When the boys arrived there they were surprised to see a huge floating dock which lay low in the water. Two seaplanes were alongside it at the foot of a steep wooden ramp. Behind the floating dock was a large stationary one, set on tall wooden pilings.

"Wow!" Joe remarked. "The tide here must rise to about twenty feet. It's at ebb now."

"Right. And at flood tide these docks must come about level."

Walking briskly, they descended the ramp and talked with a mechanic servicing one of the seaplanes.

"Is a fellow named Ted Sewell around?" Frank asked. He was told that Ted had been there the day before, but so far that day had not shown up.

"We'll come back later," Frank told the mechanic.

They walked along the waterfront, where rows of fishing boats thrust up a forest of masts.

"I guess that people in Alaska either sail or fly," Joe said.

"They have to. Roads are scarce," Frank pointed out. "You can't very well drive a car into the bush."

The boys made several more inquiries about Ted Sewell, but no one had seen him that day. They also asked a dock guard about renting a motorboat to take them to Tony's camp on the Kooniak River.

"Sure, you can rent one easily," the guard told them. "But you'll have to wait till morning and talk to the owners."

After walking up a steep hill the Hardys found themselves in front of the Alaska Historical Museum, which was open that evening. They went inside and studied the exhibits. Besides mounted birds and animals, there were Indian and Eskimo jewelry and wood carvings, bright-colored blankets, and baskets woven of fine rye grass.

"Look at this!" Joe said, pointing to a paper enclosed under glass. It was a photostat of the United States Treasury check made out to Russia for $7,200,000 for the purchase of Alaska.

"And think of all the gold that has been mined here since then," Frank remarked. "Some bargain!"

They left the museum and wandered about the city for a while, then returned to the dock.

"Eight o'clock and the sun is still high," Joe mused.

"We're almost in the land of the midnight sun," Frank said. "The clerk told me the sun won't set until eleven P.M."

The air was quite cool and held a faint aroma of fresh-caught fish mingled with the tang of mountain pines. As they stood on the dock, a motorboat came put-putting toward them. Its lone occupant was a grizzled old man. His face was heavily whiskered and he wore a sea captain's cap.

"You fellers lookin' for a boat to rent?" he shouted up to them.

Frank nodded. "That's right. How did you know?"

"Dock guard told me," the old man explained. "I'll hire this 'un out cheap. Come on down an' look it over. I'll even take you out for a spin."

The Hardys eagerly climbed down the nearest ladder to a pile of rocks near the water line. As they were about to board the boat, two shadowy figures loomed out from under the dock, grabbed the boys, and pinioned their arms in a viselike grip.

"A trap!" Joe shouted. *"Help!"*

His outcry was silenced by a blow on the head. Both boys were knocked unconscious.

CHAPTER III

Waterfront Search

FRANK was the first to revive. His feet were numb with cold, and he was biting on a wad of cloth. When he tried to move, his muscles ached.

As his mind cleared, Frank realized he was bound and gagged. Then he remembered the old boatman and the sudden assault. His attackers had roped him to one of the wharf pilings!

A few feet away Joe was gagged and tied to another dock timber. He moaned as consciousness returned.

Suddenly Frank realized their feet were in the icy water. Already the waves were lapping above their ankles. The tide was rising, and the slimy dock pilings showed the high-water mark was more than a foot above their heads!

Frantically the two boys scanned the harbor. The only movement was a fishing boat far beyond the breakwater. No one would notice their plight in the semidarkness under the dock.

Some time later, back at the hotel, Chet awoke from his nap.

"Getting dark out," he noticed, switching on the bedside lamp and glancing at his wrist watch. "Wow! Five after eleven! Wonder if Frank and Joe are back yet."

Chet opened the connecting door and peered into the Hardys' room. Their beds were empty.

He hurried to the lobby and inquired at the desk. After checking the key rack, the clerk told him that the Hardys had not returned.

"Now what do I do?" Chet asked himself. The next moment he decided that the most likely place to pick up their trail would be the waterfront. Perhaps they had met Ted Sewell there.

Striding along quickly, Chet made his way to the docks and paced along the seaplane base and rows of fishing boats.

"Frank! Joe!" he called. There was no answer.

Then Chet noticed a guard lounging against a shed, smoking his pipe.

"Have you seen two young fellows around here?" Chet asked.

The guard scratched his jaw. "Oh sure! I remember now. There was two lads here a couple o' hours ago. Asked me about rentin' a boat."

"Any idea where they went?"

The man gestured with his pipe. "The last I seen of 'em was on the dock."

Chet walked out on the pier to scan the harbor. Perhaps, he thought hopefully, his friends had hired a boat for a spin. But there was no craft in sight on the darkening waters.

As he stood wondering what to do, he heard a muffled noise. *Bump! Bump!*

The sound seemed to come from under the dock. Getting down on his hands and knees, Chet peered over the side, but he could make out nothing in the heavy gloom.

"Frank! Joe!" he called.

In response came a series of frantic whimpering noises. The eerie sounds sent a chill down Chet's spine. He jumped to his feet and ran back to the guard's shed.

"Someone's trapped under the dock!" he cried out.

"You must be imagining things, sonny."

"Oh, no, I'm not!" Chet insisted. After a brief argument, he talked the guard into launching a small dory. Still grumbling, the man rowed out along the pier while Chet aimed a flashlight among the wooden pilings.

Presently he gasped. "Frank! Joe! There they are!" By now the water was up to the boys' chests.

The guard's eyes popped. "I don't believe it!"

After jockeying the boat into position, he

whipped out his jackknife and went to work on the ropes. Chet helped him. Finally they freed the two youths and hauled them aboard.

Both Frank and Joe were numb with cold. Their teeth were chattering so hard that at first neither could speak.

The guard rowed ashore quickly and hustled the Hardys into his shed, where Chet wrapped them in blankets. The guard heated some milk on his potbellied stove. As Frank and Joe gulped the nourishing liquid, their strength slowly returned.

"What happened?" Chet asked when they were able to talk.

Frank told how the whiskered old boatman had lured them into an ambush. "I didn't get much of a look at the men who grabbed us, but I'd say they were slender and about medium height."

"Right," Joe added. "That's all I could make out, too. Their faces were masked."

"That old feller was lyin'," the guard declared. "No one asked me if you two lads were lookin' fer a boat to rent."

"He may have trailed us and overheard our conversation," Frank said. "Or maybe it was just a shrewd guess."

If the man *had* been guessing about their need for a boat, Joe reflected, this might mean he knew the Hardys were going to the Kooniak River.

"Want me to call the police?" the guard asked.

The young detectives shook their heads. "We'll let it go till morning," Frank replied. "The police probably couldn't do much tonight, and we both need a good rest."

Early the next day the boys breakfasted at the hotel, then went to Juneau Police Headquarters. The sergeant who took their report was a former Seattle policeman, who knew Fenton Hardy by reputation.

"I'll send a man down to the docks with you," he said. "Maybe he can help you spot that boatman."

A short, heavy-set detective, named Phil Grant, made a tour of the dock and seaplane base with the three boys. Grant, who was well acquainted around the waterfront, asked numerous people if they knew anyone who fitted the description of the boatman. No one recalled such a person.

"I'm beginning to think those whiskers and the cap were just a disguise," Frank commented.

Detective Grant shook his head doubtfully. "If so, we haven't much to go on, but I'll let you know if we turn up any clues."

"Thanks. We'll do the same," Frank told him.

Chet looked around nervously after the detective walked away. "Do you suppose those crooks are still trailing us?" he asked.

"Don't get jumpy." Joe chuckled. "I doubt if they'd try anything in broad daylight. Seriously, Frank, what do you think their game is?"

His brother shrugged. "Too early to answer that question. We'll know more after we've talked to Tony. But I'd say those guys who attacked us are part of a well-organized gang trying to scare us off this case."

Chet shuddered. "Well, they're doing a good job so far as I'm concerned."

"For a guy who's scared you're doing a great detective job, Chet," Frank remarked.

"You saved our lives," Joe reminded the stocky youth.

The gratitude and praise gave Chet courage. "Okay, fellows," he said. "Let's find Ted Sewell this time."

Again the three boys strolled out on the dock, inhaling gusts of the briny northern air. The harbor was bustling with activity.

Joe pointed to a motorboat slicing straight toward them. At the wheel was a husky blond youth about sixteen years old. "I wonder if that's the fellow we're looking for."

Frank called to him as he drew alongside the dock. "Are you Ted Sewell?"

"That's right," the boy replied. "You must be Frank and Joe Hardy and Chet Morton. Tony sent me to get you."

The three watched as the blond youth made his boat fast and scrambled up the ladder. They liked his friendly, open face.

"Sorry I didn't meet you yesterday," Ted apologized. "Motor trouble." He pulled a note from his pocket and handed it to Frank. It was in Tony Prito's handwriting and read:

Dear Frank and Joe:
    This will introduce my friend Ted Sewell. He's a swell guy and you can trust him completely. Please come out to my camp on the Kooniak River as soon as you can.
                          Regards,
                          Tony

"Okay," said Frank, folding up the letter. "How soon can we leave?"

"Soon as you fellows are ready," Ted replied.

"We'll need some camping gear," Joe pointed out.

"Maybe Ted can come along and show us a place to buy our outfits," Frank suggested.

"Sure. Be glad to," Ted said.

"How about grub?" Chet put in anxiously. "Will Tony have enough for all of us?"

Ted grinned. "Don't worry! You'll eat fine!"

An hour later, after loading their new pup tent and sleeping bags into the boat, the boys shoved off from Juneau. Ted steered down the Gastineau Channel between mountainous Douglas Island and the mainland, then southward along the coast.

"Nice boat you've got here," Frank remarked.

"It's part of Tony's outfit," the boy explained.

"I've just been using it these past few mornings to come to Juneau. Most of the time I scoot around in a little outboard."

"Doing what?" Joe asked.

"Beachcombing." The youth grinned. "I cruise around the beaches looking for old propellers, boat fittings, or scrap metal. Doesn't sound like much, but I earn quite a bit selling the stuff."

"Sounds like a great outdoor life," Frank said. "How's Tony getting along?"

Ted's face clouded. "He likes his work fine, but he's plenty worried. He's been having trouble on his job and— Well, you'd better wait and get the whole story from Tony. I hear he sent for you fellows because you're good at solving mysteries."

"We've worked on quite a few cases," Frank admitted.

"Then I wish you'd solve a mystery for me," Ted said seriously. "My father has disappeared."

CHAPTER IV

Cheechako Trouble

"DISAPPEARED!" Frank repeated, shocked.

"Yes," Ted said.

"Tell us what happened," Joe urged.

"Dad was working for the Fish and Wildlife Service, just like Tony," Ted began. "About two weeks ago he left Juneau on a survey trip into the wilderness to check on upstream feeding conditions for the salmon. He was due back in five or six days but he never returned."

"Was a search made?" Chet asked.

"Sure. The Service sent out a helicopter, also a ground party with an Indian guide, but they couldn't find any trace of him."

Ted bit his lip and tried to keep his voice from breaking. "They're afraid Dad may have been mauled by a bear or—or met with some other accident."

"We're sorry, Ted," Joe murmured gravely.

"Maybe," Frank added, "we can turn up a clue to your dad while we're helping Tony."

"Thanks, fellows."

The boys cruised along in silence for a while, past thick, mysterious forests of evergreen. The offshore waters were dotted with islands and the rugged coastline was notched by inlets and streams flowing out of the wilderness.

"These must be pretty tricky waters for a ship to navigate," Joe remarked.

Ted Sewell nodded. "There've been a lot of wrecks along the Inside Passage to Alaska. I'll show you one of them."

As they passed Admiralty Island, Ted pointed out a rotting, salt-bleached hulk sticking out of the water. "That was a schooner named the *Islander*," he told the boys. "It was wrecked years ago while carrying Klondike gold miners back to the States."

"What happened to the passengers?" Frank asked.

"They jumped overboard. Most of them were so weighted down with their bags of gold that they sank right to the bottom."

"I hope their ghosts don't haunt this neck of the woods!" Chet said.

Friendly banter continued until almost noon, when they reached the mouth of the Kooniak River. Flanked by dense timber on both banks, its ice-cold waters flowed clear as crystal.

"The Kooniak runs down from the northeast," Ted told his companions. "The headwaters are somewhere up in Canada." He turned the boat into the river and steered toward a small island about a quarter of a mile upstream. Ahead, they could see a plume of smoke rising from a camp-fire near a sturdy tent.

As they drew closer, a dark-haired boy rushed out and ran to the shore. He wore a T-shirt, dungarees, and leather jacket.

"There's Tony!" Joe shouted.

"Hi, fellows!" Tony called, waving his arms.

"I'm glad that he's all right," Frank said quietly as the trio waved back.

Ted brought the boat up to a small wooden dock which extended a few yards out into the water. One by one, they clambered out to shake hands happily with Tony.

"Welcome to Alaska!" Tony said, chuckling. "The forty-ninth state! Twice as big as Texas and—"

"Ten times as dangerous!" Chet cut in.

"It won't be for long," Tony went on. "Not with you fellows here to figure things out!"

"What's been going on?" Frank asked.

"Tell you about it later. Let's eat first. I figured Ted would be back about this time, so lunch is on the fire."

"Mm! That's for me!" Chet said, sniffing the appetizing aroma of pork and beans.

Ted offered to set the rustic pine table while Tony showed his friends around the camp.

"Not that there's much to show," Tony said. "You can walk around this whole island in half an hour."

The young stream guard led the way toward the upper end of the island. Aside from a few clumps of trees and underbrush, it was barren of cover, permitting a good view in all directions.

"That's one reason I'm stationed here rather than on shore," Tony explained. "This location enables me to keep a better lookout for poachers who might try entering the river."

"What's the other reason?" Joe asked.

"Bears. There are quite a few of them over on the mainland, but they never bother me here."

"Then I'm staying put on this island!" Chet declared firmly.

"Funny name, the Kooniak River," Frank mused. "What does it mean?"

"Search me," Tony replied. "It's an Indian name, I guess, but I haven't learned their lingo yet—except *cheechako*."

"What's that?" Joe inquired.

"What you fellows are." Tony chuckled. "New-comers, or tenderfeet. That's what the old-time sourdoughs used to call all the greenhorns who came up here during the gold rush."

By this time, they had reached a point facing directly upstream. Here the river formed a sparkling six-foot waterfall. The swift-flowing stream filled the air with spray as it plunged over the rocks.

"The salmon jump those falls on their way upstream to spawn," Tony said with a gesture. "I'll show you tonight."

"Why wait?" Joe put in eagerly. "Can't we see them now?"

Tony shook his head. "When humans are around, the salmon travel upstream after dark."

When the boys returned to camp, the meal was ready. Ted ladled out platefuls of beans, and everyone ate with a keen appetite. After a dessert of canned fruit and cookies, they leaned back with sighs of satisfaction.

"Now, Tony," Joe said, "give us the story of the goings-on here."

"Okay. The trouble started right after I arrived," Tony began. "A fishing boat put in at the mouth of the river, and the crew tried to bribe me to leave my post."

"Then what?" Chet asked, raising his eyebrows.

"I told them to scram," Tony said disgustedly. "If I'd left this spot unguarded, those crooks would have seined all the fish out of the river. And it's my job to see that they don't! This is protected water."

"Did you report the incident?" Frank inquired.

"Sure," Tony replied. "I sent word to the authorities in Juneau and a couple of special agents came here. They staked out undercover and kept watch for three days, but nothing happened. Then, the very night after they left, someone took some potshots at me while I was sleeping. You can see the bullet holes in my tent." He pointed to rents in the khaki covering.

"Wow!" Chet exclaimed. "You must be up against a dangerous bunch!"

"You're telling me!" said Tony. "Seems to me that ordinary fish poachers wouldn't risk a murder. The way I figured, something big must be going on and someone's awfully anxious to get me away from here. That's why I decided to send for you."

Frank and Joe mulled over this information while Ted prepared to leave in his own small outboard motorboat. The others accompanied him down to the dock and unloaded the pup tent and sleeping bags from Tony's boat.

Ted shook hands all around before shoving off. "Nice meeting you fellows," he said earnestly. "If you get a chance, I hope you can solve the mystery of my father's disappearance."

"We'll try," Frank promised.

Later, after the pup tent had been erected and the sleeping bags stowed, the Hardys told Tony about their own adventures since receiving his telegram.

"I think you're right, Tony," Joe concluded. "There's a gang behind all this, and they're after something bigger than salmon. If that spy Stransky is mixed up in it, they must be a foreign group."

Frank's eyes narrowed and he snapped his fingers. "You know, Aunt Gertrude may have given us a valuable clue!"

"What do you mean?" Joe asked.

"That missile she told us about. If it dropped in this area, foreign agents may be trying to find it before any Americans do."

"That makes sense," Joe agreed. "Maybe we've got a rocket search on our hands after all."

The afternoon passed quickly while the boys busied themselves with camp chores. At seven o'clock they ate supper, then talked over their plans until nightfall. When it was dark, Tony said, "Come on. I'll show you a real salmon run!"

The boys crossed to the west bank by boat, then made their way along the shore to the falls. The moon had gone behind a cloud, so Tony aimed his flashlight toward the cascading waters. The others gasped at the spectacle.

The river was alive with salmon! Glinting pink and silver in the beam of light, the fish were leaping and wriggling their way up the six-foot falls.

"Talk about a subway rush!" Joe chuckled. "What makes them so anxious to get upriver?"

"Sort of homing instinct," Tony replied. "When they're two to six years old, depending on the species, they head back to fresh water where they were born. Then they lay their eggs and die."

To keep from frightening the salmon, Tony used his light only in brief flashes. One of the flashes revealed a set of stone steps in the waterfall.

"It's called a ladder," Tony explained. "The Fish and Wildlife Service installs them in many streams to help the salmon make their leaps."

By the time they returned to camp, the newcomers were yawning and ready to crawl into their sleeping bags. The next morning, after a refreshing sleep, they ate a hearty breakfast of bacon, eggs, and fried potatoes. Then Frank suggested that they make a tour of the island to check for clues.

"Good idea," Tony agreed.

As they strode along, the Hardys kept constantly on the alert for any signs of a sneak visit by their enemies. Suddenly Joe let out a cry.

"Look!" he exclaimed, pointing to the ground ahead.

A fresh trail of footprints led from the underbrush down to the water and back! They had obviously been made by two persons. Frank studied the prints with keen interest and called his brother's attention to the heelmarks. Each contained a circle and star.

"The same kind of heelmark Stransky made back at the Bayport airfield," Frank commented.

"Good night! You don't mean that same guy is *here* too?" Chet burst out.

Frank shook his head. "Stransky couldn't have made both sets of prints, even if he managed to break jail. But they may have been made by men working with him or for him."

"The same guys who took those potshots at me?" Tony asked with a worried look.

Frank shrugged. "No telling, but these prints aren't more than a few hours old. Whoever made them was here on the island last night!"

CHAPTER V

A Strange Knapsack

A SILENCE fell on the campers as the full import of Frank's words sank in.

"What I'd like to know," Joe put in, "is how those prowlers got here. We would have heard a motorboat."

"I doubt if they'd have taken a chance on waking us," Frank said thoughtfully. "Seems more likely they came in a canoe."

Joe spoke up. "You could be right about that, Frank. They might even have come from somewhere upriver and portaged around the falls."

Frank nodded. "I think we should scout this whole area from the air. That would give us a chance to learn the terrain and all the streams around here."

"Swell idea!" Joe agreed. "We might even spot the enemy camp!"

Tony, whose equipment included a two-way radio, volunteered to call the Fish and Wildlife Service in Juneau. "They put a helicopter into service just a few months ago," he informed the others. "I'm sure that we could arrange a flight."

"Good! How about calling them right now?" Frank urged.

Tony did so, and the official on duty promised to send the helicopter to the island early the next morning.

That afternoon, while Tony attended to writing out some reports and Chet stretched out for a nap, Frank and Joe decided to explore the river-bank above the falls.

The two boys crossed over from the island by motorboat, then hiked northward along the rising shoreline. The ground underfoot was soft with a thick layer of pine needles and mossy vegetation.

"Feels like walking on a carpet," Joe remarked.

"Just right for moccasins," said Frank. "But I could sure do without the mosquitoes!"

When they were several hundred yards past the falls, Frank pointed through the trees to an object in the river. "Take a look at that rock out there, Joe. Pretty unusual, eh?"

Joe shaded his eyes and squinted at the curious pillar of stone. Rising almost six feet above the water, it was black and shaped like an hourglass. The spray from the rapids made it glisten in the sunshine.

"It sure is odd!" Joe agreed. "I wonder if it's a natural formation."

"Let's find out," Frank proposed.

The boys pushed through a thick grove of brush and alders which grew almost to the river's edge. Here they removed their shoes and socks, rolled up their pants, and waded out into the stream.

"Wow! This water's ice cold!" Joe exclaimed.

"Watch out for those sharp stones on the bottom," Frank said.

The black rock stood only a few yards from shore. It was smooth and weathered, showing no signs of having been chipped or chiseled into shape by tools.

"Funny how it narrows in the middle," Frank said. "Could the water alone have done that?"

"Probably," Joe mused, "it gets worn away by silt and debris when the river's—"

The words ended in a yell of surprise as Joe was suddenly knocked flat by a huge paw. With a splash, he landed in the water! Frank, whirling, saw an enormous brown bear! A menacing growl rumbled from its throat.

Before the bear could aim another blow, Frank plunged into the icy rapids. Balked, the huge beast then turned back to his first target. Joe was stunned and floundering in the shallow water. The bear's claws arced toward him in a vicious swipe! But Frank yanked his brother's arm, pull-

A menacing growl rumbled from the bear's throat.

ing him out of the way. The bear's paw missed Joe by inches!

Towing Joe with one hand, Frank swam frantically out of range. The foaming rapids threatened to sweep them toward the falls, but fortunately, the two boys were strong swimmers and finally reached the shore.

Meanwhile the bear, towering erect on his hind legs, glared at the youths. Luckily he made no move to pursue them.

"What a monster!" Joe gasped as they sank down on the bank. "He must be nine feet tall!"

"At least," Frank panted. "And I'll bet he weighs close to a ton!"

Joe shivered in his soaked clothing. "What made him so mad? I thought those fellows seldom attacked humans unless they're provoked."

"There's your answer." Frank chuckled wryly. "We *did* provoke him—by barging into his private fishing spot!"

Down on all fours again, the bear had just speared a plump salmon with one stroke of his paw. Flopping back on his haunches in the water, the huge animal devoured the fish in a few gulps.

Splat! Another salmon fell prey to his mighty paw. This too disappeared down his gullet, followed by half a dozen others in quick succession. At last, his hunger satisfied, the bear lumbered out of the water and vanished among the alders.

"Whew!" Joe let out a whistle of relief. "I'm sure not sorry to see that baby leave!"

"That makes two of us," Frank murmured. "Let's get back to camp before we freeze in these wet clothes!"

Dripping and shivering, the Hardys trudged along the riverbank.

"Hold it!" Joe exclaimed, stopping suddenly. He bent down and plucked a battered knapsack out of the underbrush. "I wonder who lost this."

"Take a look inside," Frank suggested. "Maybe there'll be some clue to the owner."

Joe unbuckled the straps and groped inside the pouch. "No. It's empty," he announced, holding the bag open for Frank to see.

"Wait a minute! I think there's an extra thickness of leather in there." Frank took the knapsack and ran his fingers around the interior. "Sure enough! There's a secret pocket!"

Joe looked on as Frank removed the contents. There were two items. One was a piece of jade, carved in the likeness of a fierce-looking bird. The other was a crumpled piece of paper.

"A map!" Frank exclaimed, unfolding the paper.

"Of what?" Joe stared in puzzlement. The map, crudely drawn, showed a river or stream of water and various other geographical features. But it bore no place names.

"Maybe Tony will recognize it," Frank said. "Come on. Let's go!"

Frank and Joe hurried back to the camp. Chet and Tony greeted the two bedraggled figures in astonishment.

"Do you always go swimming with all your clothes on?" Tony asked in jest.

"Only when we tangle with bears," Frank replied and told of their close call. Chet grew pale.

"We found something on the way back," Frank said, and displayed the knapsack and contents. "Have a look at this while we get some dry clothes."

As the boys changed, Tony produced a map of the area from among his gear.

"This sketch doesn't jibe with any of the places on my map," he reported.

"The jade carving doesn't add up, either," Joe said thoughtfully. "Matter of fact, I've never heard of jade being found in Alaska. Have you?"

The others shook their heads. "It certainly doesn't look like any of the Indian carvings we saw in the museum," Frank replied.

"If you ask me," Chet said, "this knapsack could have been left there as a trap. I don't think you should have brought it back to camp. It certainly could mean another visit from our enemies!"

"It's possible," Joe said, "but on the other hand, it might be a valuable clue!"

"How long do you think it had been lying there?" Tony asked, half inclined to agree with Chet.

Frank scrutinized the knapsack closely, turning it inside out and running his fingers over the material. "Not too long," he finally replied. "See, the buckles aren't even rusty!"

Joe shrugged. "It still doesn't mean someone left it there on purpose for us to find."

But Chet had grown very apprehensive by now. He looked around nervously. "I'll bet someone's spying on us right this minute!"

CHAPTER VI

Nightmare!

THEY crouched quickly and glanced about. Then Frank broke into a grin. "Cut it out, Chet. Quit scaring us like that!"

"Just the same," Joe declared seriously, "there might be something to what Chet says. I think we'd better tell Juneau about that knapsack."

Tony cranked up the aerial of his radio, turned on the set, and spoke into the microphone. "Kooniak to Juneau!"

Presently a voice crackled: "Juneau to Kooniak. Over."

Tony reported the finding of the knapsack. The department operator promised to inform the police by telephone and then to call back.

A few minutes later his voice came over the speaker. "The police say that no such loss has been reported. But our pilot will pick up the knapsack for them when he flies out with the helicopter."

"Okay, thanks," Tony said. "Over and out."

After a hearty supper the boys washed their mess kits and talked for a while around the campfire. When they were ready to retire, Chet seemed nervous.

"I still think we may get a return visit from that gang," he insisted. "How about standing watch tonight?"

"Okay. That's not a bad idea," Frank said. "Let's draw straws to pick our turns."

Joe won the first assignment. Chet, Frank, and Tony would follow in that order. It was broad daylight through most of Joe's watch. Finally, yawning, he woke Chet.

As the plump youth took over, the birdcalls became hushed. The sky flamed red, then a deep brooding twilight settled over the pine forest.

"These woods are positively spooky at night!" Chet thought. Selecting a comfortable spot, he sat down under a tree. "No use getting nervous. I'd better think of something cheerful!"

Determinedly Chet concentrated on visions of himself salmon fishing—pulling in one silvery fish after another. This made him feel better.

Night deepened. Soon it was completely dark, except for the circle of light around the campfire. From across the river came the melancholy hoot of an owl.

Chet, lulled by the peacefulness of the night, settled himself more comfortably against the tree. "This isn't such a bad spot after all," he thought drowsily. The next instant he sat bolt upright and a horrified yell escaped his lips. The Hardys and Tony awoke in a flash and came rushing out of their tents.

"Chet! What's wrong?" Frank cried out.

The boy was on his feet, trembling. "S-s-something came at me out of the darkness!"

"You mean an animal?" Tony asked.

"No—men! A whole gang of them! They tried to club me, but I fought them off!"

"*What?*" Tony stared at him. "You must have been dreaming! There's no one around here but us!"

"But I saw them, I tell you!" Chet insisted, still shaking with fright. "Masked men!"

Frank and Joe quickly scouted the ground around the camp. But there were no footprints or other trace of intruders.

"Exactly where did all this happen?" Frank inquired calmly.

"Right here," Chet replied. "I was sitting with my back against this tree, and all of a sudden—"

"You fell asleep," Joe broke in, chuckling, "and had a nightmare!"

To reassure their friend, the Hardys and Tony took lanterns and made a thorough search. Finally Chet agreed that he must have dreamed the whole incident.

"Go ahead and hit the sack," Frank told him with a grin. "It's almost time for my watch."

At breakfast the next morning Joe and Tony ribbed Chet about his wild dream. He took their jokes good-naturedly, adding, "At least these flapjacks are real. Slip me a few more, Frank!"

Breakfast over, they busied themselves with their morning chores. Soon after they finished washing up, the helicopter arrived from Juneau.

"I'm Robbie Robbins," the pilot said. He was a pleasant young man, sandy-haired, about twenty-two years old.

The boys shook hands and explained why they had sent for him. Then Frank showed him the crude map which the Hardys had found in the knapsack. "Ever seen a place like this?"

Robbins studied the map and shook his head. "Not that I recall. But there are so many lakes and streams around here that I wouldn't want to say for sure. We'll keep our eyes open."

The helicopter had seats for three besides the pilot, but Chet elected to stay on the island with Tony. "You do the exploring," he told Frank and Joe. "I feel safer on the ground!"

Robbie and the Hardys climbed aboard, and the helicopter took off. Soon the Kooniak appeared as a ribbon of blue winding among the evergreens. The pilot headed northward, working back and forth in widening sweeps across both sides of the river.

"I don't see any place that looks like this map," Joe remarked.

"No sign of a camp, either," Frank said as he scanned the terrain with binoculars.

Several hours later the boys noticed a cluster of huts about a mile west of the Kooniak. "It's a Haida village," Robbie told the Hardys. "They're one of the Alaskan Indian tribes."

"Could we land and question them?" Frank inquired. "I'd like to find out if they've seen any strangers lately."

"Okay. But you may not find them very talkative," Robbie warned.

The helicopter descended slowly to the village clearing. Instead of running to meet their visitors, the Indians gathered to watch from a distance. Their dark, slanted eyes, set in coppery faces, stared impassively at the newcomers.

"They don't look very friendly," Joe muttered.

"Do they speak English?" Frank asked the pilot.

"Most of them do, although they may not admit it. Often they use the Chinook trading jargon in talking to strangers."

The Indians made no move so the pilot stepped forward. *"Klahowya!"* he said in a loud voice. Several men of the village returned his greeting.

"We're looking for some white men," Frank

told them. "Have you seen any strangers around here?"

The Indians merely shrugged and shook their heads. "Looks as though we're not going to get much out of them," Robbie murmured.

"Let's circulate around the village," Frank suggested. "Maybe they'll open up a bit after they get used to us."

Robbins agreed, so the trio strolled around, peering at the Indian dwellings. Though crude, the houses were stoutly built. Near each one stood wooden racks, with strings of fish drying in the sun.

Frank and Joe were intrigued by a number of small log structures, poised on stilts as high as a man's head. There was one beside each house, with a ladder going up to the entrance.

"What are those things?" Joe puzzled. "Oversized birdhouses?"

Robbie Robbins grinned. "No, they're caches," he explained, "for storing food out of reach of wild animals."

Several Indian children trailed around behind the white visitors, watching them curiously. Finally one teen-age boy grew bold enough to speak.

"I'm Fleetfoot," he said to Frank.

"Glad to know you." Frank offered his hand, hoping to make friends with the boy. "I'm Frank Hardy. This is my brother Joe, and this is Robbie Robbins."

After pumping each one by the hand, the Indian youth continued, "You ask about strangers?"

"That's right," Frank said. "Have you seen any recently?"

"*Nowitka!* Yes," Fleetfoot replied. "One day I went to the river to fish. Saw two white men drift downstream in a big canoe. They talked a lot."

"Did you hear what they were saying?" Joe asked eagerly.

The Indian boy paused, furrowing his brow as if trying to remember the exact words. "I heard one man say, 'They protect the salmon. The salmon protect us.' Then the other man said something in strange lingo—not like American talk. I didn't understand it."

Joe shot an excited glance at his brother, who said, "Fleetfoot, will you do something for us?"

"Maybe." The Indian boy smiled and shrugged. "What do you want?"

"Next time you see those men, or any other strangers, trail them to their camp—but keep out of sight, so they don't see you. Then come and tell us. We'll be staying on the island at the mouth of the river."

The boy looked uncertain.

"Maybe we can do something for you. What would you like?" Frank asked.

A broad grin spread over the young Indian's face. "I'd like to ride in the whirlybird."

Robbie Robbins chuckled. "Okay, it's a deal, Fleetfoot."

Satisfied with the results of their visit to the Indian village, Robbie and the Hardys took off again in the helicopter.

"Frank, it looks as though our guess was right," Joe said excitedly. "If one of those men spoke a strange language, we must be up against foreign agents!"

"It sounds that way," Frank agreed. "But I sure wish we knew what they're after. Let's hope Fleetfoot delivers on his end of the bargain!"

Continuing northward, the helicopter soared above the rolling foothills of the Alaskan coastal range. Beyond the timberline, the rocky slopes towered up to snow-capped peaks. One of the mountains drew Frank's attention by its strange contours.

"Gosh, look at that," he remarked, pointing out the unique formation to Joe. "Those peaks stick up just like four fingers and a thumb."

"A good description," Robbie put in. "The Indians call it Devil's Paw, and you can see why." He added, "That whole range up ahead forms the international boundary between Alaska and British Columbia. Guess we'd better turn back."

On the return trip, Robbie circled over an enormous tongue of ice, seventeen miles long. Glittering blue-white in the sunshine, it trailed down from the mountain snowfields almost to the coast.

"Mendenhall Glacier," the pilot told Frank and Joe. "It's actually a river of ice."

The boys gaped at the spectacle. "A river?" Joe echoed. "You mean it flows?"

"Yes, but so slowly you could never tell by the naked eye," Robbie replied. "I guess *creeps* might be a better word."

Suddenly Frank exclaimed, "Go lower, Robbie! I think there are two people down there!"

The helicopter swooped toward the glacier. "You're right!" Joe cried. "A man and a woman! They must be stranded!" The tiny figures signaled frantically, waving their arms. They appeared to be seated on the ice.

"Can we rescue them?" Frank asked the pilot.

"We'll sure try!" Hovering into position above the two people, Robbie told the boys to unreel a rope ladder which he carried in the rear of the helicopter's cabin.

At sight of the ladder, the man on the glacier shook his head and signaled with his arms.

"He wants someone to climb down and help them," Frank said. "I'll go!"

CHAPTER VII

Glacier Trek

THE helicopter hovered lower over the ice as Frank prepared for the rescue. Easing himself out of the cabin, he groped for a footing on one of the metal rungs. The ladder swayed sickeningly as he climbed down. But Frank kept a steady grasp. Finally he reached the glacier. The middle-aged couple, dressed in hiking garb, greeted him with anxious relief.

"Sorry to put you to so much trouble. We're certainly grateful that you responded to our signals!" The man, although he seemed to be in pain, flashed a smile. "My wife and I had an accident. Our name's Turner. I'm an engineer."

Frank introduced himself, and Mrs. Turner, a pleasant-faced woman, added her thanks.

"We've had a nasty fall on the ice," she explained. "I'm afraid my husband's leg is broken, and I seem to have sprained my arm quite badly. Could you possibly take us aboard?"

"Of course, Mrs. Turner." Frank smiled reassuringly. After studying the situation, he removed two rungs of the ladder and improvised a splint for Mr. Turner's leg. Then he lashed first the woman, then the man, to the ladder and had them lifted aboard.

"There won't be room for all of us," Joe told the pilot. "Suppose I keep Frank company on the glacier while you take Mr. and Mrs. Turner to the hospital?"

"I guess that's the best plan," Robbie agreed. He reached into a storage locker and took out two pairs of steel cleats. "Here. You and Frank fasten these to your shoes. They'll help you keep your footing on the ice. I'll be back pronto to pick you up."

"Okay, thanks." Joe pocketed the cleats, and after wishing the Turners a speedy recovery from their injuries, climbed down the ladder. Then Robbie reeled it back aboard. The two boys waved as the whirlybird took off toward Juneau.

"This is a chilly-looking spot, all right," Frank remarked, gazing around at the vast expanse of ice. "What a nasty place to have an accident!"

"You said it!" Joe replied. "Which reminds me —we'd better put these on before we take a spill ourselves!"

He handed Frank one set of cleats, and they sat down on the ice to attach them to their shoes. Feeling a bit more sure-footed, they decided to do a little exploring while they waited for Robbie's return.

"Let's have a look farther up the gorge," Frank suggested.

"Suits me—if we can make it." Joe took a couple of trial steps, moving as gingerly as a man walking on eggs. "Boy, it's a good thing Robbie gave us these cleats, or I'd be flat on my back by now!"

Frank chuckled. "Keep your fingers crossed. It could still happen!"

In appearance, the glacier was more like a mountainous ridge than a river. Its surface was humped and uneven, as well as split with cracks and fissures. The boys made their way along slowly, enjoying the majestic view of the mountain slopes that rose on either side of the glacier.

Suddenly Frank let out a yell as he lost his footing. "Joe! Help!"

Joe threw himself flat on the ice and caught his brother by the arm in the nick of time. An instant later Frank would have slid into a yawning crevasse!

"Whew!" Frank lay panting for a moment after Joe had pulled him to safety. "That was too close for comfort! I didn't even notice that downslope till I hit the skids!"

"Maybe we'd better head for shore," Joe suggested. "This berg is too tricky to navigate."

"Second the motion!"

By the time they reached the timbered slope on the nearest side of the valley, a chill wind had sprung up. Blowing down from the mountains, it rustled the branches of the tall evergreens.

"I'm glad these fir trees act as a wind screen," Frank remarked with a shiver.

"Right now, I'd prefer the kind of furs we could wrap around us!" Joe retorted wryly.

As the moments of waiting dragged by, both boys began to feel hunger pangs from having missed lunch.

"Could I go for a square meal!" Joe groaned.

"Don't look now, but here comes someone with the same idea!" Frank pointed to a huge prowling bear which had just appeared among the underbrush, a hundred yards away.

"Oh—oh!" Joe turned pale. "I suddenly lost my appetite! Come on! We'd better return to the glacier!"

The Hardys hastily retraced their steps. After peering in their direction for a while and sniffing the air hungrily, the bear ambled off into the timber. The boys heaved sighs of relief.

"Think it's safe to go back?" Joe asked.

"Let's not tempt him!" Frank cautioned.

"W-w-what's keeping Robbie?" Joe muttered, his teeth chattering from the cold. More than an hour had passed.

"Search me," Frank replied. "It's not a long

run to Juneau. Maybe he was delayed at the hospital."

Both boys were chilled to the bone and ravenously hungry when the drone of a plane's motor finally reached their ears. Shading their eyes against the dazzling sun glare, they saw a small single-engine craft wing into view. It flew in low above the treetops and circled overhead.

"The pilot's signaling us!" Joe cried out.

The Hardys waved back.

"He's going to drop something," Frank said as they saw the cabin door open. The pilot shoved out a large package, and it plummeted to the ice a short distance away.

The boys rushed to examine it. "Let's hope it's food!" Frank exclaimed.

Frank cut the twine with his jackknife and tore off the heavy wrapping paper. Inside were a pair of sheepskin coats rolled around a cardboard box. The box, warm to the touch, proved to contain roast-beef sandwiches, two Thermos bottles of coffee, and a note from Robbie Robbins, which said:

> *Dear Frank and Joe:*
> *The copter is laid up for repairs but here's something to keep you going. After you've eaten, start walking toward the mouth of the glacier. I'll send a car to meet you.*
> *Robbie Robbins*

Frank read the note with a slight frown. "Tough break," he commented.

"Never mind, let's eat!" Joe said cheerfully. "My mouth's watering!"

The boys waved their thanks to the pilot, still circling overhead. He rocked his wings in response and flew off. Frank and Joe donned the sheepskins gratefully, then tackled the sandwiches with gusto. Their spirits rose with every bite.

"Man, those tasted wonderful!" Joe said as he swallowed the last mouthful. "Almost as good as Mom's or Aunt Gertrude's!"

Frank agreed and finished his coffee. "Let's get going. We've got a long trip to the mouth of the glacier."

Greatly invigorated, the Hardys began their trek. At first they enjoyed the rugged grandeur of the mountain scenery. They were snug in their warm sheepskins, and the brisk wind blowing down from the glacier made their blood tingle.

"When summer vacation started, I never thought we'd wind up hiking on ice!" Joe remarked with a chuckle.

"We should have brought skates," Frank added with a grin.

As the afternoon wore on, however, the boys began to feel the effects of the dangerous journey. Their leg muscles ached from the constant strain of keeping their footing on the ice.

"What say we try it over on the side of the

valley again?" Frank suggested. "That bear's probably found himself another snack by now."

"We *hope!*" Joe quipped. "But okay. It can't be any worse than this."

Back on dry land, the boys found the going easier, in spite of the tumbled rocks and heavy underbrush. Nevertheless, the hours of steady trudging proved a grueling ordeal. By the time they reached the gravel road connecting with the Glacier Highway that led to Juneau, the Hardys were exhausted.

"Joe, hold it a minute. My foot hurts," Frank said. "I think I've got a whopper of a blister." He took off his shoe and examined his foot.

"Whew! What'd I give to be hitting the sack right now!" Joe groaned, sprawling full length on the ground.

"Let's hope we don't have to wait too long for that car," Frank said, with a glance at his wrist watch.

"What time is it?" Joe asked.

"Eight minutes before seven."

By nine o'clock the car promised by Robbie had not arrived, and the boys were getting cold.

"Joe, it'll be dark in two more hours," Frank said uneasily. "I think we should start walking toward town. Doesn't look as though that car is going to show up."

"Okay. But I'd sure like to know what's behind the delay!"

Wearily the boys set out. The sun went down and gradually dusk began to gather. A plane droned overhead, followed by a weird bird screech from the forest. Otherwise, the Alaskan wilderness seemed wrapped in silence. On and on the boys trudged, with the same harrowing thought in mind:

Had Robbie fallen victim to the Hardys' enemies, bent on preventing their rescue?

CHAPTER VIII

Salmon Raid

THOUGH becoming more tired and footsore every minute, Frank and Joe plodded on toward Juneau. Finally they reached the outskirts of the city, where they flagged a taxi.

"You fellows look bushed," the driver remarked as they climbed in. "Where to?"

"The seaplane base," Frank said.

At the dock they questioned a guard about Robbie Robbins. He told the Hardys that both the pilot and his helicopter were gone. "Robbie took a passenger with him," the man reported. "Told me he was going to pick up two boys on Mendenhall Glacier."

"But we were told the copter was laid up for repairs!" Joe exclaimed. "A plane dropped us a note to that effect."

"Robbie did have some trouble with his copter," the guard conceded, "but that was five hours ago. Say, are you the two fellows he was talking about?"

"That's right," Frank declared. "The note said that he'd send a car for us, but it never showed up. Neither did the copter."

"How'd you get to Juneau?"

"We walked."

The dock guard shoved back his cap and scratched his forehead. "That's funny." A troubled frown spread over his weather-beaten face. "Hanged if I can figure it out! Didn't you sight his copter on the way?"

The boys shook their heads, and Joe asked, "Who was his passenger?"

"A man," the guard replied, "but I didn't get much of a look at him, only from a distance. By thunder, I hope nothing's happened to Robbie! He may have had an accident!"

The Hardys were equally concerned, although they refrained from mentioning their fears of foul play. "Any chance of sending out a plane to look for him?" Frank asked.

"Sure! The bush pilots around here always keep a search plane on standby." Much perturbed, the dock guard bustled into his booth and made a phone call to arrange a take-off early in the morning.

Realizing there was nothing more they could do, the Hardys hurried to the Baranof Hotel and checked in for the night. Too tired even to think of food, they tumbled into bed.

The next morning Frank and Joe returned to the seaplane base. To their dismay, there was still no news of Robbie, nor had his helicopter been sighted.

"We'd better notify the police," Frank decided. "Then I vote we head back to the island."

At police headquarters Detective Grant jotted down the details of their story and promised to send out an alert to all authorities in the state. "We still have no lead on that gang who ambushed you at the dock," he added. "But if Robbins has met with foul play, it may be the work of the same group."

After promising to keep in touch, the boys left headquarters, pausing outside to discuss their plans. "We'll have to get ourselves a motorboat," Joe decided.

"And a canoe, too," Frank suggested. They had little difficulty renting a trim-looking craft. The owner also provided a sturdy canoe, which they attached by a towline to the motorboat. They embarked and headed down the Gastineau Channel. Eager to reach the island, Frank ran the boat at full power for most of the trip.

As they neared the mouth of the Kooniak, the distant sound of gunfire reached their ears.

"Shots!" Joe exclaimed. "Tony and Chet must be in trouble!"

Frank nodded grimly. Jerking the throttle wide open, he sent the motorboat roaring ahead through the choppy water. Its bow leaped clear of the waves, showering the Hardys with spray.

As they rounded a point and turned into the river, another rifleshot cracked—then another! Frank and Joe stared in dismay. A man, in a small speedboat piloted by a companion, was sniping at the occupants of the island. Tony and Chet had apparently dodged for cover among the trees. Meanwhile, three boatloads of fishermen were hauling in wriggling masses of salmon with huge nylon seines.

"Those crooks!" Joe gritted between clenched teeth. "They couldn't bribe Tony, so now they're using bullets to keep him out of action while they pull off their salmon raid!"

"Even those seines they're using are against the law!" Frank added. Suddenly he whipped the boat around in a fast turn.

Joe, startled, exclaimed, "Hey, what's the idea?"

"We can't stop them single-handed," his brother pointed out, "but perhaps we can get help. I don't think they have spotted us yet."

"We can't go all the way back to Juneau," Joe said.

"No, but I'm hoping this boat may be equipped with a radio. Take a look in the rear locker!"

Joe did so and let out a jubilant yelp. "You're right! A two-way set! I'll warm her up!"

In a few moments he had the set sputtering and crackling. Not knowing the proper frequency for either the Juneau police or the Fish and Wildlife Service, Joe left the tuning untouched while he issued a few trial calls over the microphone. Almost immediately a ham operator responded.

"This is Luke Burton near Ketchikan," the voice said. "Come in, please."

Joe explained the situation, and Burton replied, "Poachers, eh? Just stand by and I'll raise Juneau in a hurry. They'll have the law down there so fast those guys won't know what hit 'em!"

The boys cruised out of sight beyond the point to await developments. Burton was as good as his word. Presently the drone of aircraft was heard, and two seaplanes came swooping down to a splash landing in the mouth of the river.

Joe gave an exuberant whoop. "Let's get in there and watch the fireworks!"

Grinning, Frank steered the boat back into the Kooniak. Armed enforcement agents were already covering the poachers with carbines and barking out orders through megaphones. Sullenly the fishermen emptied their seines, then brought their boats alongside the waiting planes.

The speedboat, hemmed in between the waterfall upstream and the patrol planes at the mouth of the river, was also forced to surrender. An agent went aboard each of the fishing craft, and the speedboat was taken in tow.

"Are you the fellows who radioed the alarm?" the officer in charge asked the Hardys as Frank maneuvered within speaking distance.

"We contacted a ham near Ketchikan," Joe explained through cupped hands. "He relayed word to Juneau!"

"Nice work!" the man called back. "Come on ashore and we'll see what these poachers have to say for themselves!"

As the Hardys approached the island, they were relieved to see Tony and Chet running to greet them.

"You guys all right?" Frank asked as he and Joe climbed out on the little wooden dock.

"Sure, thanks to you two!" Tony replied. "But things were getting mighty hot with those bullets kicking up dirt around us!"

"I thought it was curtains for us!" Chet gasped, still shaking with excitement.

"Why didn't you radio for help when those men first showed up?" Joe asked.

"I tried to," Tony explained, "but another radio kept jamming my signal. I judge it was a powerful set and not far away. After that, the snipers started shooting at us and we headed for the trees. I didn't get another chance to send."

Meanwhile the enforcement agents were herding the poachers ashore for questioning. There were nine in the group, including the two from the speedboat. The men were unshaven and rough-looking. They faced their captors with sullen expressions.

The agent in charge, who knew of the previous attempt to fish the Kooniak, asked Tony, "Have you ever seen any of these men before?"

Tony studied them with an uncertain frown. "No. Sorry, but I don't recognize any of them."

One hulking fellow, evidently the ringleader, spoke up. "You can't pin anything else on us! This is the first time we ever fished around here!"

"Your last time, too!" the agent snapped. Then he advised the prisoners of their rights.

"What about those bullets which were fired at Tony's tent?" Frank put in. "Maybe we can make a ballistic comparison," he suggested, hoping that one of the group might be panicked into confessing.

But the sniper snorted scornfully. "Go ahead and compare! Them bullets won't fit *my* gun!"

The poachers also denied having any part in Robbie Robbins' disappearance, or in jamming Tony's transmitter. The latter claim seemed borne out by the fact that there was no radio equipment in any of their boats capable of jamming a broadcast signal.

After the prisoners and agents had left, the four

boys gathered around the campfire to talk over the events of the past two days.

"I'll make us some hot dogs," Chet volunteered. "A fellow needs something to keep up his strength after an experience like that!"

"At least it hasn't affected your appetite," Joe teased. "Not that anything could!"

Tony reported that he and Chet had had no trouble up to the time the raiders appeared. Then Frank and Joe told about their visit to the Haida village, their adventure on the glacier, and their forced trek into Juneau. Their two friends listened with keen interest. Tony was especially intrigued to learn about the Indian boy's report of seeing two strange white men in a canoe.

"Those fellows *must* be mixed up with the gang," Tony remarked, "because they never showed themselves in the open around here."

"Maybe they didn't come this far downriver," Chet put in.

"Where else would they be going?" Joe argued. "Frank and I didn't spot any camp between here and the Indian village. And we looked hard!"

"What puzzles me is that short-wave jamming," Frank mused. "Try your set now, Tony, and see if you get a clear signal."

Tony did so, and was able to contact Juneau without any difficulty. After the boys had finished their hot dogs, they strolled toward the north end of the island.

"I'd sure like to know if those salmon poachers had anything to do with the jamming," Frank went on.

"They had no equipment," Joe reminded him.

Frank admitted this, adding, "But I'm sure it just wasn't a coincidence that the jamming occurred at the same time as their raid."

Conjecturing broke off suddenly as Tony yelled, "Look!" and pointed upstream.

A lone figure, standing upright in a canoe, was about to plunge over the falls!

CHAPTER IX

Fleetfoot's News

In seconds the foaming rapids would sweep the canoeist to disaster!

"His boat will be swamped!" Joe gasped. "Come on! Let's help him!"

The boys raced to the dock to launch their canoe. But they halted in amazement as the other craft took the plunge over the falls like a graceful sea bird!

"Hold it!" Frank called out. "That fellow doesn't need help!"

"It's Fleetfoot!" Joe exclaimed.

Balancing himself with his paddle, the Indian boy shot through the spray and landed, still upright, at the foot of the falls. Then he paddled toward the island.

The boys hurried down to the shore. "You really gave us a scare, Fleetfoot," Frank told him.

The Indian grinned. "Don't worry. White water is fun! Sometime I'll teach you how."

In spite of the ease with which he had shot the falls, Fleetfoot seemed to be bursting with inner excitement. "I have a message and have come for the whirlybird ride!"

"I'm sorry, Fleetfoot," Frank explained. "You may have to wait for your ride. The copter is missing, and so is the man who owns it."

The Indian lad's face darkened with disappointment. "You mean—you break your promise?"

"Now hold on, Fleetfoot," Frank said gently. "I'm speaking the truth. Yesterday, after we left your village, Robbie, the pilot, went to Juneau and picked up another man. All we know is that he flew away and never came back."

Fleetfoot stared first at Frank, then at Joe, as if trying to read their minds. He said nothing.

"We'd like you to help us find him," Joe urged.

This seemed to convince Fleetfoot. "All right," he said slowly. "I believe you." After a short pause, he added, "I saw the whirlybird yesterday."

"You mean you saw it *again*, after we left your village?" Frank asked eagerly.

"It flew over the village. Went that way," the Indian said, pointing northeast.

Joe looked at his brother and whistled. "Toward the Canadian border!"

"Wherever they went, I'll bet Robbie didn't

fly there willingly." Frank frowned. "His passenger may have forced him deep into British Columbia. They even may have crashed in the wilderness."

Joe mulled this over. "I think your first guess is right, Frank," he conceded. "This gang we're up against probably doesn't dare take any chances on the police catching up with them. I'll bet they're holding Robbie prisoner."

Frank snapped his fingers. "Do you suppose Mr. Sewell is being held prisoner too—by the same gang?"

"I'll bet you're right," put in Tony. "From what I hear, Mr. Sewell was an experienced woodsman. A tenderfoot might have run into trouble in the wilderness, but not an expert who's been working here for years."

Frank went on thoughtfully, "If this gang *is* a foreign group looking for that lost rocket, they could probably use a guide."

"Could be," Joe spoke up. "But for all we know, Robbie's passenger might have been a United States scientist who hired him to make an aerial search for the rocket; or a detective or FBI agent trailing the gang."

Suddenly Frank remembered that Fleetfoot had come with a message. Turning back to the Indian boy, he asked, "What is the news you have for us?"

Fleetfoot smiled proudly. "I saw the same two men on the river again last night."

"Did you follow them?"

"Part way," the boy said. "They went upriver past Devil's Paw into British Columbia. I cannot go there without identification. That is against the law. I think maybe those men broke the law. Maybe they stole something and ran away."

The Hardys received this new information with keen interest. Frank patted the Indian boy on the shoulder. "Many thanks, Fleetfoot. You've done good work. If you find out anything more, please let us know. And I promise you'll get that whirlybird ride as soon as Robbie shows up!"

The Indian grinned. "If I find out more, I'll be back!" He shoved his canoe into the water, leaped aboard nimbly, and waved farewell. *Klahowya!*"

The boys watched as Fleetfoot paddled across to the mainland, beached the canoe, and hoisted it for the portage around the falls.

As the Hardys headed back to camp they considered their next move. "We sure can't cover all this bush country without a helicopter," Frank said. "Our best bet is to return to Juneau to see if we can line up another whirlybird. Maybe the Fish and Wildlife Service can help us."

Joe agreed, "There might be some news about Robbie, too."

The Hardys left their canoe on the island and started back to Juneau in the rented motorboat. The skies, which had been blue and clear when they embarked, gradually darkened with scudding storm clouds.

"We're in for a blow," Joe observed.

"Maybe we can outrun it," Frank said, increasing speed. However, as they left Admiralty Island astern, the wind grew to gale force. It lashed the waves into breakers, hurling spray high into the air. The Hardys' boat, battered by wind and water, was almost swamped.

Joe bailed frantically. "Can we make shore?"

"Not a chance!" Frank replied as he fought to keep the boat on course. "If we try leaving the channel, we'll pile up on the rocks for sure!"

The rain held off for almost half an hour. Then lightning flashed and a peal of thunder seemed to split the heavens wide open, sending the rain down in a torrent.

The boys, soaked to the skin, redoubled their efforts to keep the boat from swamping. They bailed in shifts, one taking a turn at the wheel while the other scooped out buckets of water.

The storm pursued them up the Gastineau Channel, but gradually abated as they neared Juneau. Both boys were shivering and exhausted when they finally tied up at the dock. By this time it was past ten P.M. and almost pitch dark.

"Guess we may as well check in at the hotel," Frank advised. "We can't do anything before morning."

The Hardys' boat was almost swamped.

The boys had a hot supper in their room at the Baranof, then turned in and slept until seven the next morning. After a hasty breakfast of bacon and eggs, they hurried down to the seaplane base. When they learned that there was still no news of Robbie Robbins they were disappointed.

"Is there any other copter around here beside Robbie's?" Frank asked the dock guard.

"Not in Juneau," the guard informed them.

"Let's query the Fish and Wildlife Service," Frank suggested. "Perhaps they can get us a whirlybird from Ketchikan or Skagway."

Their visit to the government office, however, proved to be futile.

"Nearest copter's at Anchorage," the agent said. "We tried to charter it ourselves, but the pilot's tied up for the next three weeks."

Before returning to the island, Frank and Joe also checked with Detective Grant at police headquarters. The Hardys told him they planned to search the upper reaches of the Kooniak for traces of the foreign gang, as well as for Sewell and Robbins. "Will we need permission from the Canadian government?" Frank asked.

"Yes," the detective replied, "but I can arrange it." He called the Canadian consulate and quickly got an okay. Their permission was extended to include Fleetfoot, as well as Ted Sewell and Chet, in case the latter two decided to accompany the expedition.

"Thanks a lot," Frank told the detective as they shook hands. "Can you give us any tips about traveling in British Columbia?"

"Never been up that way myself," Grant replied, "but I'll tell you someone who should know. He's an old-timer named Jess Jenkins. You'll find him at the Alaskan Pioneers' Home in Sitka."

The boys boarded a small commercial plane and within an hour were on the lawn that surrounded the Pioneers' Home in the former Russian capital of Alaska. They found Jess Jenkins sunning himself in front of the building.

The old fellow proved to be a lean, bewhiskered sourdough who had mined gold in both Canada and Alaska.

"Sure," Jenkins said, when questioned by the young sleuths, "I know what's up there in British Columbia! But I warn you, it's even more dangerous than a hoppin'-mad Kodiak bear!"

CHAPTER X

The Sourdough's Clue

FRANK and Joe seated themselves on either side of the old sourdough so as not to miss a word of his warning.

"Ah, them was great days," Jenkins reminisced. "We figgered it might pan out almost as rich as Joe Juneau's strike."

The Hardys flashed each other puzzled glances. "What would pan out?" Frank asked.

"Why, this gold strike I'm tellin' ye about," Jess replied. "Over into Canady, it was. Seems two fellers come down the Kooniak, luggin' full bags. Pretty soon the story spread around about them stumblin' on these gravel bars, up some little crick, where the color was runnin' forty dollars to the pan!"

"When was this?" Joe put in.

"Well, let's see. More'n fifty years ago, I reckon." The old sourdough fell silent for a moment. Finally he went on, "Anyhow, folks in Juneau got all het up, hearin' about this new strike. So a bunch o' us boys hightailed it over into British Columbia to stake out claims."

"What happened?" Frank pressed curiously.

"Trouble, that's what happened!" Jess retorted. "An' that's what I'm warnin' you boys about. We found the spot, an' then got chased right out again by a bunch o' wild Indians!"

"Why?" Joe asked.

" 'Cause this crick, where the gold was supposed to be, run right past a sacred Indian burial ground. Seems as how all their ancestors had been buried there. They knew we'd start sinkin' shafts all over the place, an' they didn't take to that idea. So naturally we had to clear out."

"You never went back?" Frank asked.

"Nope. We figgered we'd rather hang onto our scalps for a while. But some o' our boys got a peek at one o' them graves."

"You mean they dug one up?" Joe asked.

"Well, no. What I mean is they got a peek at one o' the grave houses. Little bitty log houses, they are, 'bout six by ten feet. That's where they stored the Injun's weapons an' other gear over his grave."

The old sourdough rambled on, talking about his experiences in the wilds of British Columbia, the Yukon, and Alaska. The Hardys listened attentively. When they finally said good-by, Jess told them, "Come again any time, boys," and gave each a hearty handshake. "Always glad to talk about the old days!"

Frank and Joe walked away thoughtfully from the Pioneers' Home. "Was there *really* a gold strike up there?" Frank mused. "And Indians? I wonder if they're still there."

Frank frowned as they walked toward the seaplane basin. "Maybe those two men didn't really strike gold after all. They could have looted the grave houses of valuable Indian jewelry and ornaments."

"And then traded them off for gold?" put in Joe, sensing the drift of his brother's reasoning.

"Yes, and when rumors started about how they made their haul, it touched off a gold rush."

"I'll bet you're right!" Joe said enthusiastically. "That might explain the jade trinket we found in the knapsack!"

"Exactly," Frank agreed. "Furthermore, someone may have recently stumbled on the burial ground and unearthed more treasure."

They had a half-hour wait for the return flight to Juneau, so Frank and Joe sat on a bench at the base of a huge totem pole that overlooked Sitka Harbor.

"There's one thing that doesn't fit in with your theory," Joe said after a few minutes of silence.

"What's that?"

"Where would those old Indians have obtained jade? It comes from Asia, mostly."

"True enough," Frank said. He added, however, that many scientists believe the Indians came originally from Asia. If so, they might have brought their tribal treasures with them.

"In that case," Joe exclaimed, "the jade ornament may be valuable scientific evidence!"

Joe's exuberance was interrupted by the distant drone of motors. A plane was arriving from Juneau and would soon take off on the return trip.

Minutes later the plane was air-borne. It skimmed over the mountainous islands of the coast and landed on Gastineau Channel. The Hardys hastened to the hotel for their belongings, then purchased a large quantity of fresh supplies. They hauled them down to the dock, loaded them into the motorboat, and headed back to the island.

Upon arriving, Chet and Tony said that they had been frantic with worry during the night.

"We were afraid you might have cracked up in the storm!" Tony said.

"Besides, we had a scare of our own!" Chet added.

"What happened?" Frank asked.

Tony explained that they had heard the sound of paddling close to the island shortly after the storm abated. Tony had flashed his searchlight but failed to pick out any canoeists.

Joe grinned. "Are you sure you weren't hearing things?"

"We weren't sure then, but we are now," Chet retorted firmly. He ducked into the pup tent for a moment, and came out holding a well-worn paddle. "Take a look at this. We found it on the beach this morning."

The paddle had obviously been hand-carved. "Indian workmanship," Frank speculated. "Perhaps Fleetfoot can identify it."

Then Joe went on to tell of their plan to explore farther along the Kooniak. "We feel sure that the gang must be operating somewhere up-river," he said. "I'm hoping we can locate Robbie and Mr. Sewell, too."

"That could be plenty dangerous," Tony pointed out. "Suppose you run into another ambush?"

"They're not apt to lay a trap for us unless they know we're coming," Frank replied. "If we watch our step and keep our eyes open, we may be able to spot their camp without being seen."

"Especially since we're taking Fleetfoot with us," Joe put in.

"Too bad Ted Sewell isn't here," Frank remarked. "We figured he might want to come along to hunt for his dad."

"Stick around for another twenty-four hours," Tony urged. "Ted ought to show up pretty soon."

The Hardys agreed to wait at least until the

following morning. The delay proved worthwhile because Ted arrived on the island that evening.

As the boys sat around the campfire, Ted reported glumly that he still had had no word on his father. He was amazed to hear about the latest developments, and when Frank told about their plans, he eagerly agreed to go.

"I've always wanted to take a trip into British Columbia!" Ted said. "We'll need rifles and ammunition, though. That's bear country!"

Though Frank and Joe had been carefully trained by their father in the proper use of firearms, they never carried weapons when working on detective assignments. However, since they already had had two brushes with bears they could see the wisdom of Ted's advice.

"I guess you're right," Frank agreed. "But Joe and I don't have guns."

"I have a Springfield that I bought from Army surplus," Ted informed them. "Makes a swell hunting rifle! Maybe that'll do for the bunch of us. But you fellows should have some practice before we leave."

After supper the boys set up a row of empty cans on rocks. Ted then brought out his rifle, which he carried in his boat, as well as several clips of ammunition. To his amazement, both Frank and Joe proved to be excellent marksmen, drilling their target cleanly on every shot.

"You don't need practice!" Ted exclaimed.

Frank grinned. "Our dad's a pretty good teacher."

The rest of the evening was spent in discussing the details of their river trip. It was decided that after picking up Fleetfoot at the Haida village, they would follow the Kooniak at least as far as the Indian grave houses.

The next morning Tony insisted that he would be all right alone on the island. But Chet decided to stay with him. "In case there are any more gun-happy fish poachers around, you'd better have company," he declared.

Then Chet suggested they pick some blueberries for breakfast. The others agreed eagerly. While Tony heaped wood on the campfire and started the bacon frying, the Hardys, Chet, and Ted hiked across the island. On the way Chet suddenly let out a cry of delight.

"Hey, look! Wild celery!" He reached down, pulled up one of the leafy green stalks, and started to bite into it.

Ted paled. "Chet! Stop!" he yelled.

CHAPTER XI

A Fiery Missile

WITH a lightning grab, Ted yanked the stalk out of Chet's mouth before his teeth could sink into it.

"Hey! What's the big idea?" Chet protested.

"That stuff isn't celery," Ted explained. "It's deadly poisonous water hemlock!"

"Poisonous!" Chet gulped and clutched his throat.

"Don't let it spoil your breakfast," Joe comforted him. "We'll pick those blueberries and do some real eating."

Chet cheered up at this appetizing prospect, and the boys soon returned to camp with a fine haul of berries. After breakfast Tony radioed the Fish and Wildlife Service for news of Robbins and Sewell.

"No word on either of them yet," Tony reported as he took off his earphones. "But the operator passed on a message from the Bayport police."

"What is it?" Joe shouted.

"They've learned that Romo Stransky has a twin brother named Remo—and *he's* a spy too!"

"Hear that?" Chet crowed triumphantly. "I told you I wasn't seeing things! Remo must be the one I saw at Seattle-Tacoma airport!"

"He probably followed us to Juneau, too," Joe declared. "What's more, he may have left those star-and-circle heelmarks here on the island."

Frank went even further with a deduction. "I'll bet Remo was Robbie's passenger!" The others agreed. As they prepared for the trip upriver, Frank went on, "You know, fellows, if we're lucky enough to find the helicopter, we might be able to fly it back."

"Not if the gas tank's empty!" Joe cautioned.

"It most likely will be," Tony said. "But you could carry enough fuel in the canoe to get the copter back to Juneau."

Ted Sewell looked doubtful. "The canoe will be plenty loaded as it is, with all our duffel."

"You're right," Frank agreed. "We'd need an extra canoe."

"Which means another trip back to Juneau," Joe pointed out.

In spite of further delay, Frank's companions realized his suggestion was a wise one. "Okay," Ted said after a short discussion. "We're all in favor. Let's draw straws for the job."

The task fell to Ted and Joe. They embarked in the Hardys' motorboat and headed up the coast. When they arrived in Juneau, the boys purchased as many tins of gasoline as they thought could be safely carried.

On Ted's suggestion, they also stopped at a sportsmen's outfitting store and bought two rifles for Frank and Joe. After the supplies had been loaded aboard, Joe rented another canoe which he fastened to the stern of the motorboat.

They were having sandwiches and milk at a nearby lunch counter when Joe suddenly set his glass down hard.

"Something wrong?" Ted asked.

"Wow!" Joe exclaimed. "Why didn't I think of that before?"

Ted looked baffled. "Of what?"

"The Turner couple Robbie rescued from the glacier," Joe replied in a low voice. "They might know something about his mysterious passenger."

Ted brightened. "That's a good hunch, Joe! Come on!"

The two boys hurried to the Juneau Hospital, where Joe inquired whether they might see Mr. and Mrs. Turner. The receptionist nodded pleasantly and consulted a card file. "They're in Room 214. You may take the elevator."

In Room 214 Joe and Ted found William Turner in bed, with his leg in a cast. Mrs. Turner, her right arm in a sling, was seated in a chair reading to her husband. Both were delighted to receive visitors.

After Joe introduced Ted, Mrs. Turner said, "So nice of you to come. Where's Frank?"

Joe explained. Then Mr. Turner said, "Hope you boys didn't wait long on the glacier before the pilot returned."

"As a matter of fact, he never did get back," Joe replied.

The couple looked dismayed. "Oh, I'm terribly sorry!" Mr. Turner said. "Robbins' copter developed some kind of trouble on the way to Juneau. But he told us it could be fixed."

Joe gave them the details of Robbie's disappearance.

"Oh, dear!" exclaimed Mrs. Turner. "I wish we could help!"

"Perhaps you can," said Joe. "Do you know anything about his passenger?"

The couple thought in silence. Joe prodded their memory. "Did you see anyone speak to Robbie when you landed at the seaplane base?"

"Only a couple of mechanics who were working nearby," Mrs. Turner replied. "One of them called an ambulance for us."

Joe then asked whether they had noticed anything suspicious on their glacier expedition.

"I'm afraid not," Turner replied. "You see,

ever since I retired three years ago, Clara and I have made a hobby of paleontology."

Ted was interested to hear this. "I guess there are a lot of prehistoric animal bones around our Alaskan glaciers," he remarked. "I know prospectors have come across the remains of ancient woolly mammoths. But I've never seen any myself."

Forgetting his unfortunate accident, Turner brightened and talked about the finds he and his wife had made. "As a matter of fact," he went on, "we believe the earliest life on this planet developed right here in North America."

"The first human beings too?" Joe asked.

"That's hard to say," Turner replied. "However, I think the Indians originated on this continent."

"I thought they were supposed to have come over from Asia."

"That's the opinion of most scientists," Turner conceded. "Personally, I believe it was the other way around. They probably trekked from here to Asia via the land bridge over the Bering Straits. Later, they traveled back and forth."

"Is there any evidence to support that theory?" Joe asked.

"Yes, a great deal. There are similarities between the American Indians and Asiatics both in features and customs. Also, they both used the bow and arrow, and have many common root words in their language."

Excitedly Joe queried, "How about their ornaments and jewelry? Is there any chance the Alaskan Indians might have brought jade carvings back from Asia?"

Mr. Turner nodded. "Very possible, I should say." After hearing about the boys' planned trip up the Kooniak River, he said, "Why not keep alert for traces of prehistoric animals? You might stumble on some valuable finds."

"What should we look for?" Ted inquired.

"Well, a white streak in gray rock might indicate a bone fossil," Turner replied. "Or a depression in the rock could be a dinosaur's footprint. Either one could lead you to a prehistoric skeleton."

"We'll remember that!" Joe promised as the boys got ready to leave.

They quickly strode to the dock and shoved off in the heavily laden motorboat, with the canoe trailing behind.

As soon as they reached the island, Joe told Frank of the conversation at the hospital. Frank was pleased to learn that the Turners supported his theory about the jade piece.

Not long after supper, the boys turned in, hoping for a good night's sleep before embarking up the Kooniak next morning. Soon the camp was wrapped in silence.

But Frank was restless. Turning and tossing in his sleeping bag, he kept reviewing in his mind the baffling events that had happened since the Hardys had arrived in Alaska.

"Were those fish poachers mixed up in this mystery?" he asked himself. "And what about Robbie? . . . Looking for that gang in this wilderness may turn out to be a lot more difficult than we bargained for."

Unable to sleep, Frank rose and pulled on his slacks, socks, and loafers. The luminous hands on his watch pointed to 12:20. He strolled toward the water, listening to the sighing of the night breeze in the tall pines.

Suddenly another sound broke the stillness— the soft splash of an oar, then a clink of metal containers rattling against one another! Frank strained his eyes in the darkness, every sense alert. He spotted a man in a boat. The next second he shouted:

"Wake up, fellows! Someone's stealing our canoe and gasoline!"

As Frank raced toward the dock, Joe, Chet, Ted, and Tony burst out of their tents and sprinted in their bare feet. Too late! The noise of a motor roaring into action told them the intruder was making a clean getaway!

Reaching the water's edge, Frank saw their canoe and gasoline untouched! The raider's boat kicked up a violent wake as it streaked off. Suddenly the strange man stood upright and hurled something toward the island. As the object struck the little wooden dock next to the canoe, it burst with a dull thud and yellow flames shot high into the air!

Frank's face blanched in the blinding glare. "It's a fire bomb!" he yelled.

CHAPTER XII

Dinosaur Detective

"TONY, get some axes!" Frank commanded as the dock burst into flame. To the others he cried, "Follow me!"

As Tony dashed back to camp, Frank kicked off his loafers and plunged into the water. With his jackknife, he slashed the lines holding the boats.

"Chet, take our motorboat! Ted, grab yours!"

Joe, meanwhile, was frantically attaching the canoes by towlines to the crafts. "Okay! Take off!"

Chet and Ted revved up their motors and sped into the middle of the river. The Hardys, seared by the heat from the fiery dock, beached Tony's boat at a safe distance, then hastily scrambled ashore.

Tony was already hacking at the dock timbers. "There's an ax and a hatchet for you fellows!" he called.

Half the wooden structure was a crackling mass

of flames. Shielding their faces as best they could, the three boys quickly cut away the remaining supports. Then Frank levered up the planking with his ax.

"Okay! Into the water!" he gasped.

Straining every muscle the trio ripped up the flimsy structure and hurled it into the water. It sank with a hissing cloud of steam. Panting and streaked with perspiration, the boys watched as the flames died out.

"Wow!" Tony muttered. "If that fire had spread to the brush, our whole camp would have gone up in smoke!"

Once the danger was past, Chet and Ted returned with the boats and canoes. These were moored to the blackened stumps of the dock pilings. Then all the boys trudged back to camp.

"Good thing you were awake, Frank," Ted remarked wryly.

"We should have kept up our night watches," Joe added. "Tony, I think you and Chet need more protection after we three leave the island."

"Let's report the incident to Juneau," Frank suggested.

"I'll do it right now," Tony replied.

Warming up his radio, he tuned to the agency's special frequency and spoke into the microphone: "Kooniak to Juneau! . . . Do you read me?"

Fortunately the station kept an operator on duty around the clock. After hearing Tony's report of the fire-bomb attack, he consulted his superiors by telephone, and then called back. "We'll send out two men first thing in the morning!"

Much relieved, the five boys drank some hot cocoa which Chet had brewed. Ted volunteered to stand the first watch during the remaining hours of darkness. Then the others crawled into their sleeping bags. The rest of the night passed quietly.

Shortly before ten o'clock that morning a boat arrived at the island, bringing the two agents from Juneau. They came ashore, carrying a small but powerful two-way radio set, which they turned over to the Hardys.

"The chief thought this might come in handy on your trip up the Kooniak," one of the men explained. "If you get a lead on the gang, he'd like you to report to Juneau at once."

"Thanks. We'll do that," Frank promised.

Half an hour later the Hardys and Ted set off, paddling to the western shore of the river. Here they unloaded the two canoes and made the portage around the falls.

"Whew! That's a full day's work before we even get started!" Joe remarked, wiping the perspiration from his brow.

Ted chuckled. "These Alaskan rivers are beautiful, but you'll find they're no picnic to navigate!"

After a brief lunch the boys embarked on the next leg of their journey. Frank volunteered to paddle the trailing canoe which carried the gasoline cans.

Ted approved. "We'll ride better that way, with one man behind. And there'll be no danger of losing the fuel tins in an upset."

Ted, as the most experienced woodsman of the trio, took the bow position in the lead canoe. They shoved off, and soon found themselves paddling against a swift current. They were also traveling "uphill" since the Kooniak flowed down from the Alaskan coastal range.

"Boy, looks as though we're in for a real workout!" Joe called back to his brother. Frank grinned in response.

"Don't worry, you two are in good shape," Ted commented. "This would be rough for a tenderfoot."

At points along the riverbanks the heavy timber thinned out into lush meadowland, carpeted with wild flowers in every color of the rainbow. Frank and Joe were amazed at the dazzling display.

"It's like a giant garden!" Joe said admiringly.

Ted pointed out many of the species by name —alpine forget-me-nots, fireweed with its tall reddish spires, yellow Arctic poppies, bluebells, creeping dogwood, and purple irises.

Steering close to shore, he reached out and plucked several flowers from a mass of yellow blooms that grew down to the water's edge. "Monkey flowers," he told Joe.

"They do look like little faces," Joe said with a chuckle.

After paddling for several hours, they reached an area where the banks of the Kooniak rose in rocky walls. The beetling cliffs formed a canyon for the swift-flowing icy waters.

"Hey, look!" Joe cried suddenly, pointing up at one of the cliff faces. "There's a white streak in the rock! Could it be part of a dinosaur?"

When Joe suggested investigating the streak, Ted and Frank agreed to moor the canoes and accompany him.

"It'll be a tough climb, though," Ted warned.

"We can make it!" Joe urged enthusiastically.

They tied their canoes to a clump of rock, climbed out, then began scaling the cliff. Footholds were few. After skinning their arms and legs on the rugged outcroppings, they finally reached the whitish streak.

"I'm sure it's a bone!" Joe exclaimed.

All three examined it closely.

"Could be," Ted agreed. "But how do we get it out?"

"By the Indian method," Frank suggested. "Chip it loose with a sharp stone."

Arming themselves with chunks of flint, the boys followed Frank's suggestion. Gradually more of the white object was revealed.

"I was right!" Joe exclaimed. "It's definitely a bone!"

"Looks like some kind of an elbow or knee joint," Ted commented. "If dinosaurs had such things!"

"Wait till I get back and tell Mr. Turner about this find!" Joe said jubilantly.

Frank broke into a chuckle. "I bet he'll give you a medal!" he joked.

As the boys started down toward the canoes, their smiles faded. The steep cliff, which had been so difficult to climb, seemed almost impossible to descend.

Suddenly Joe gasped as he lost his footing. With a yell, he slid downward, making frantic attempts to slow his descent.

CHAPTER XIII

A Savage Ordeal

TED acted instantly! Leaping out from the cliff, he dived into the water far below. After a few strong strokes, he reached the rocky shore and climbed to the foot of the slope.

Joe, tumbling and twisting, was almost at the bottom of the cliff. In the nick of time Ted caught hold of Joe, breaking his fall just short of a jagged rock formation.

The impact threw both boys to the flinty ground, where they lay panting and trembling for a few moments.

"Whew!" gasped Joe. "How can I thank you, Ted! Finding that dinosaur bone came close to killing me! If it hadn't been for you, my own bones would be in pretty bad shape by now!"

"Just a lucky catch," Ted said with a grin.

Even so, Joe had suffered many bruises and his skin was scraped raw in several places.

Frank, who had tensely watched the rescue,

shouted, "I'll find a safer place to come down."

By climbing higher and crossing a shelf of rock to a point farther upriver, he was able to make the descent in safety.

Ted, meanwhile, had opened their first-aid kit and applied medication to Joe's cuts.

"I never knew fossil hunting could be so dangerous!" Frank quipped wryly as he rejoined the other two.

"You can say that again!" Joe muttered, blowing on a particularly painful cut on his right knee.

After resting for fifteen minutes, the trio resumed the trip upriver. Although they watched both banks carefully, the boys saw no one, white man or Indian.

Toward evening they approached a small, wooded island in mid-river.

"Let's camp here," Frank suggested. "It should make a pretty safe spot for the night."

After paddling into a small cove, the travelers beached the canoes and scouted the island thoroughly before unloading their gear.

Soon a campfire was crackling and the aroma of hot corned beef and fried potatoes drifted over the island. After supper the boys chose watch periods. Joe drew the first assignment. Frank and Ted stretched out in their sleeping bags and were soon asleep. All were thoroughly refreshed by daybreak, although Joe was still somewhat stiff and sore.

Breakfast over, the canoeists pushed on. An hour of paddling brought them to an open spot on the west bank, where the clustering pines gave way to a narrow clearing.

"Hold it!" Ted cried, signaling with his paddle. "That's an Indian trail!"

"It might lead to the Haida camp," Joe conjectured.

Frank was certain of this. "Let's go ashore and get Fleetfoot," he urged.

"Think our gear will be safe here?" Joe asked as they drew the canoes up on the riverbank.

"Better not take any chances," Frank replied. "I vote we cache our supplies and each of the canoes in a separate spot."

Joe and Ted concurred, and in twenty minutes the boys had everything well hidden under heaps of brush and rocks. Then they headed inland along the trail. Soon they came upon the Haida village.

As they neared the cluster of wooden huts, the sound of excited voices reached their ears. A crowd of Indians were swarming about the village clearing.

The boys stopped short in astonishment at an amazing sight. A woman, wearing a green fringed parka, shot straight upward at least thirty feet above the crowd! She was treading air to remain upright!

Seconds later, she landed on both feet in a

walrus skin held by six men. They immediately snapped the hide taut and catapulted her up in the air again!

"Good night!" Joe gasped. "What do they think she is—a human medicine ball?"

A slender young Indian turned at the sound of Joe's voice. It was Fleetfoot. He ran toward them with a wide-eyed look of fear. "Quick! Do not let my people see you!" he whispered. "Run for your lives!"

The boys looked puzzled, and Frank said, "Why? Your tribe was friendly enough the other time we came to your village."

"Today we are having a wedding," Fleetfoot explained. "That woman is the bride. She is a Kotzebue Eskimo, and now she is proving to everyone that she will be a good, *skookum* wife!"

"By letting them bounce her on that walrus hide?" Joe asked.

Fleetfoot nodded impatiently. "It is a custom of her people. And today any outsiders who come here must do the same! But it takes much practice. You would break your neck!"

"Wow!" Ted gulped. "We'd better clear out of here! Come on!"

But the boys tarried too long. Hearing their voices, the Indians swarmed toward them excitedly. Before the Hardys and Ted could take to their heels, they were dragged into the circle of yelling, whooping Haidas!

Joe gasped. "What do they think she is—
a human medicine ball?"

"Hey, wait a minute!" Frank pleaded, striving to make himself heard above the uproar.

"When white men come to village, they must join in wedding games too!" a brave asserted. He pointed to Frank. "This one is biggest, looks plenty strong. He will try test with walrus hide!"

The brave explained the rules. Frank would be bounced in the air three times. If he managed to land upright after three tries, he was *skookum*.

Frank stared at the speaker unbelievingly.

Ignoring the protests of Joe, Ted, and Fleet-foot, the Indians seized Frank and hustled him onto the walrus hide. Then the hide was raised aloft and snapped taut. Frank went hurtling high in the air!

He tried frantically to tread air with his hands and feet as he had seen the woman do. But the dizzying momentum of his flight upward seemed to rob him of his sense of balance. Twisting help-lessly, Frank plummeted back toward the walrus hide and landed on his back with jarring force.

Stunned, he struggled to his feet. The Indians gave him a moment's respite, then again hurled him aloft!

Joe and Ted watched, wide-eyed and helpless. For a second, Frank seemed to be dancing on air. Then, thrashing violently, he came down again, this time landing on one side.

Badly shaken, Frank managed to stand up. His last chance! Although his heart was hammering, he gritted his teeth, determined not to fail. Once more the Indians catapulted him.

Joe could scarcely bear to watch. Ted clutched his arm in breathless suspense.

Arrowing straight upward, Frank closed his eyes, keeping his arms close to his sides. As he reached his highest point in mid-air, he opened his eyes again. The circle of Indians stood far below, gaping up at him, the walrus hide seeming not much bigger than a handkerchief.

Frank felt himself begin to fall, slowly at first, then at higher speed. He stretched out his arms and trod the air gently, like a man on a unicycle. It worked! He landed squarely on both feet, still upright!

The crowd roared its approval! Frank was lifted off the walrus hide, hoisted onto the shoulders of two Indians, and paraded about the village clearing amid whoops and yells.

"You *skookum* fella!" The Haida chief beamed when he was finally allowed to stand on his own feet again. "Now you and two friends all come to the wedding feast!"

"Thanks," Frank replied, a trifle weakly. Joe and Ted, then Fleetfoot, wrung his hand in congratulation.

"Terrific!" Joe told his brother.

"I just kept thinking of what else they might do to me." Frank grinned.

"It's a wonder you could think at all after those first two jolts!" Ted exclaimed.

The villagers now gathered about a great central campfire. Two medicine men performed a religious dance, then the chief joined the hands of the Indian groom and his Eskimo bride. The wedding feast followed.

Squaws brought huge carved wooden platters heaped with food. The first course consisted of slabs of pink salmon.

"Good night! It's raw!" Joe whispered.

The boys took some, however, in order not to offend their hosts, and managed to eat a few bites. The bear steaks and stewed rabbit which followed were more to their liking. These were accompanied by nuts, berries, vegetables, and fruits, including one with a citrus flavor, which tasted like a cross between lemon and grapefruit. Ted identified it as the fruit of the wild rose.

"Boy, now we're getting fancy!" Joe chuckled as he sampled the fruit's delicate flavor.

There was also something that looked like coarse baked bread. "Wonder what it's made out of," Frank muttered, after trying a few bites.

Fleetfoot explained, "Women make flour by grinding up bulbs of rice lily." He pointed to some brownish-purple flowers which several of the squaws wore in their hair. "Those are flowers from the same plant."

When the feast was over, the Hardys at last

found an opportunity to tell Fleetfoot about their trip upriver. Frank asked if the Indian youth would accompany them as guide.

"I'd be glad to come with you!" he explained. "But I'll take my own canoe. It is much better than white man's."

"Fine! Let's go!" said Joe.

But Fleetfoot looked shocked. "No, no!" he told the boys. "Not now. The wedding party is just beginning!"

"Just beginning?" Frank echoed uneasily.

"Sure. There's singing and dancing to come," Fleetfoot explained. "We'll go tomorrow morning."

The Hardys and Ted looked questioningly at one another, trying to conceal their feelings of impatience at the further delay. However, there was nothing to do but yield. Settling back, they prepared to watch the proceedings.

Soon tom-toms beat. The medicine men started a slow, stately dance, shaking wooden rattles. As the tempo increased, the other Indians joined in and the squaws chanted steadily. The three visitors found themselves absorbed in the ceremony, despite the delay in their journey.

"Whew!" Joe exclaimed in wonderment. "How long can they keep on dancing?"

Fleetfoot smiled broadly. "Oh—Indians love to dance. They never get tired."

Gradually, as shadows gathered on the forest,

the white boys became drowsy. One by one, Joe, Ted, and Frank all dropped off to sleep.

When they awoke, it was daylight. Fleetfoot was shaking them. "Come on! We'll start now!" he said.

The Hardys and Ted returned to the river and uncovered the gear which they had cached. They loaded the supplies, then the canoes were launched.

Fleetfoot disappeared long enough to get his own birchbark canoe, which was beached farther downstream. A few minutes later he came into sight, paddling with smooth, graceful strokes.

As he drew alongside, Frank said, "There's something we meant to ask you, Fleetfoot. The other night a carved wooden paddle was washed up on our island at the mouth of the river." When Frank described it, a strange expression of fear and awe passed over Fleetfoot's face!

CHAPTER XIV

A Suspicious Campsite

"FLEETFOOT looks as if he's seen a ghost," Frank thought.

The Indian boy asked slowly, "Did the paddle have cuts in the handle?"

"Yes," Joe spoke up. "Two small rounded gouges."

Fleetfoot fairly trembled. His eyes grew wide. "That paddle was made before the white man came! Even before my grandfather's grandfather was born!"

"You mean back in the days of the ancient Athapascan Indians?" Ted asked.

"Yes! Yes! It was left on the beach by the spirit of an old Indian!"

"I doubt it," Frank said thoughtfully.

"So do I," Joe chimed in. "There were live men paddling around the island that night. Probably the same bunch we're looking for."

Ted was eager to push on, so they started upriver. This time, Joe rode the trailing canoe which carried the cans of fuel.

After pausing briefly for lunch, they continued their journey upstream. Frank and Joe, whose arm muscles had ached at the end of the first day's canoeing, gradually found themselves swinging their paddles with the same smooth, easy rhythm as Ted Sewell and Fleetfoot.

Presently Ted pointed ahead to their left. "There's Devil's Paw!" he called out.

The weird outcropping of rock loomed against the mountainous skyline like four fingers and a thumb sticking up in the air.

Fleetfoot paddled close to the other canoes. "This is a bad place," he confided. "Old men of my tribe say the devil carved it from rock. Indians do not go there."

"In that case," Joe mused, "it would make a perfect hideout for the gang. Indians would stay away from it, and the average white man would have no reason for going there."

Frank nodded. "You're right. We'd better investigate."

At first Fleetfoot objected, but as soon as he realized that the boys were not frightened by the old Indian tales, he conquered his fear. Moreover, the prospect of stalking criminals filled him with keen anticipation. His Indian blood rose to the challenge.

After running their canoes ashore, the searchers cached their crafts and provisions for a second time.

"Take your rifles," Ted advised tersely. Each of them shoved a clip of cartridges into the magazine of his firearm and stuffed more into pockets before setting off on the rugged trek toward Devil's Paw.

Carrying their weapons in one hand and clutching at trees and shrubs with the other, the four made their way up the steep slope. From time to time one of them missed his footing, sending a shower of rocks and gravel clattering toward the river.

"We'll never take the gang by surprise at this rate!" Joe grumbled, pausing to wipe the sweat from his eyes.

After half an hour of hard climbing, they reached a point where Devil's Paw and the entire surrounding terrain stood out in clear view. But there was no sign of a campfire, nor any other trace of human beings.

"Maybe we've been wasting our time," Ted said, discouraged.

"We can't be sure," Frank replied, "without making a closer search."

Now, however, the approaches were so steep that it was impossible to climb farther. Tired and disheartened, the boys retraced their route to the canoes.

"If the gang is really using Devil's Paw for a hideout," Ted remarked, "they must have some easier way of getting to it."

"Right," Joe said, removing a pebble from his shoe. "There must be a secret trail somewhere."

Fleetfoot spoke up eagerly. "You wait here. I'll go look for the trail."

"Hey! Wait!" Frank called out.

The boy did not seem to hear. He darted nimbly up the mountainside, and was soon lost to view among the scrub evergreens and underbrush.

Frank, Joe, and Ted waited, sprawled comfortably on spongy pine needles among the rocks. All were glad of a chance to rest. As time passed, however, they gradually became uneasy. More than an hour had gone by since Fleetfoot's departure.

"Wonder what's keeping him," Frank glanced at his watch for what seemed like the hundredth time.

"Let's hope he didn't stumble into the gang," Joe remarked.

"We should have given him one of the rifles," Ted said gloomily.

The words were hardly spoken when the underbrush parted and Fleetfoot stepped into view, a wide grin on his coppery face.

"I found the trail!" he reported proudly. "The

ground showed a lot of footprints. Looks like men went back and forth many times!"

"How about their camp?" Joe asked eagerly. "Did you find where the trail led?"

"Yes. But no one was there. Let's get the canoes and go up the river," he urged. "Then we can look here again on the way back."

Frank and Joe rejected this suggestion. Being good detectives, they were determined to follow through on their plan, leaving no stone unturned in their search for clues.

"You've done fine, Fleetfoot," Frank told him. "But we'd like a look at that campsite ourselves. Will you take us to it?"

Fleetfoot agreed willingly, and after gathering up their rifles, the other three youths followed him. He led them upriver for a short distance, following a twisting route among the trees and rocks. Then he turned left, up a narrow draw.

"Now you can see the trail." Fleetfoot pointed to a well-beaten path. It sloped gently up the mountainside by easy stages.

"Nice work, Fleetfoot!" Joe congratulated him. Bending close to the ground, he added, "Frank, here are more of those star-in-circle heelmarks!"

Pressing forward up the trail, they found the campsite. It lay at the base of one finger of Devil's Paw. Here again were many of the odd heelprints, as well as the blackened ashes of a recent campfire. A number of empty, discarded food cans had also been tossed carelessly aside.

"Pretty sure nobody would ever find this spot, weren't they?" Joe commented.

"Are you positive none of the gang is lurking around?" Ted asked Fleetfoot.

"No one here," he replied confidently. "I scouted for strangers before I came up the trail."

"The question now," Frank said, "is whether they're coming back? And if so, how soon?"

"Let's take a look around while we're up here," Joe suggested. "We might spot a smoking campfire."

He led the way as they followed the shelf-like rock which rimmed the base of Devil's Paw. The ground sloped away below in a steep, brush-covered incline.

Rounding a corner of the weird finger-and-thumb rock formation, Joe stopped suddenly and looked down. "Hey! Come here quick!" he yelled to the others, beckoning frantically.

CHAPTER XV

The Singing Wilderness

STARTLED by his brother's shout, Frank looked up, barely in time to see Joe suddenly drop out of sight.

"Oh no!" Frank exclaimed. Fleetfoot and Ted rushed to his side, then all three climbed to the spot where Joe had just been standing.

In utter amazement they stared down a long, rocky slope. *At the bottom lay a helicopter.* Joe was scrambling toward it.

Near the edge of a barren, desolate area of forest-tufted rock formations, the wide-spreading branches of a tall cedar effectively concealed the craft from the air. The boys' vantage point, however, gave them an unobstructed view.

"Come on, fellows!" Joe yelled up the steep mountainside. "Let's see if Robbie's anywhere around!"

Frank, Ted, and Fleetfoot followed eagerly. Grabbing for a handhold on any rock or clump of shrubbery that offered a grip, they made their way down the incline at breakneck speed.

Joe was already examining the helicopter as they approached. "The fuel tank's empty," he reported. "No sign of Robbie, either."

A weird silence lay over the desolate scene. Except for a hawk circling overhead, there was no other indication of life. While Ted and Fleetfoot watched curiously, the Hardys subjected the helicopter to a careful scrutiny.

"At least there's no blood or signs of a struggle," Joe commented. "That may mean Robbie is still safe."

Frank asked Ted and Fleetfoot to stand guard over the helicopter while he and Joe investigated the surrounding wilderness for clues. "Keep an eye up there toward Devil's Paw," he added, "in case the gang comes back."

"Okay," Ted replied. "You fellows watch your step, too. If any of that bunch *are* around, they might try to spring an ambush."

Gripping their rifles firmly, the Hardys began combing the terrain around the helicopter in widening circles. The silence was broken only by the scuffing sound of their footsteps among the brush and gravel. A lone birdcall suddenly echoed among the pines, then died away in a twitter.

"Boy, this place is eerie!" Joe muttered.

"It's hard to believe *any* human being was ever here!" Frank said.

Not a footprint or broken twig gave the slightest indication of recent visitors to the area. Overhead, the hawk was still soaring and circling in search of prey.

Suddenly Frank stopped short and clutched his brother's arm. "Joe!" he hissed. "Do you hear something—or am I imagining things?"

"Hear what?" Joe inquired. Then his questioning look gave way to an expression of blank amazement. "It's *music!*"

The strains of a dance orchestra wafted faintly through the wilderness!

"Must be a radio playing somewhere," Joe said finally.

"But where?"

Stiffly tense, the Hardys looked cautiously about. Were members of the gang hidden nearby, watching every movement? Was a trap about to be sprung on them? Hearts pounding and eyes alert, Frank and Joe walked on, holding their rifles cradled at the ready. They poked into the underbrush and peered among the trees.

"The sounds are coming from over there," Frank said, pointing to a formation of granite boulders.

The boys approached cautiously, fearful of a

possible trap. They scouted around the rocks, but saw nobody. Neither was there any sign of a radio.

Abruptly the music died away. A few seconds later the Hardys were electrified to hear a voice speak clearly in a foreign language! But neither Frank nor Joe could identify any of the words.

Then a second voice replied—this time in English: "The salmon are going up the river. The bears will have a feast." As the voice finished speaking, the music resumed.

"What do you make of it?" Joe asked his brother, completely baffled.

Suddenly an idea occurred to Frank. "Wait a second! Let's check some of those other rocks!"

They put their ears to several boulders. All were broadcasting the music. Frank snapped his fingers excitedly.

"Joe, I've got it! Somehow these rocks are acting as natural receivers and picking up a broadcast signal! I've read about cases like this before! Remember that man in Newark who picked up broadcasts in the fillings of his teeth? It nearly drove him crazy."

"That must be the answer," Joe agreed. "But I still don't understand how it happens."

"Neither do I, exactly," Frank admitted. "It has something to do with their resonating frequency, I guess, just like a crystal detector. Maybe there's something about these rocks that intensifies the signals, too. Anyhow, I think we're getting the gang's broadcast."

"No doubt about that," Joe replied. "The voices that broke in didn't sound like commercial announcers or ordinary radio hams!"

"Those words in English must have been in code," Frank went on.

"You're right!" Joe exclaimed. He conjectured further about the reference to salmon. "It ties in with what Fleetfoot overheard on the river."

"And," Frank said thoughtfully, "I didn't like the remark about the bears having a feast."

"What do you mean?"

"The salmon going up the river may refer to us," Frank explained. "And 'the bears will have a feast' could mean our enemies are laying a trap."

"Good night!" Joe stared at his brother in dismay. "That makes sense, all right! But what can we do about it?"

Frank shrugged. "Just keep our guard up, I guess. Come on," he added. "Let's go back."

By the time the Hardys returned to the helicopter, the music had ceased. But Ted Sewell and the Indian lad were still tense with alarm at the strange sounds of the "singing wilderness." They, too, had heard the broadcast, although much more faintly than Frank and Joe. Fleetfoot was frightened at what seemed to him to be spirit noises.

"Devil's Paw is a bad place, I tell you!" he kept repeating. "Evil spirits live here!"

Frank reassured him, explaining the strange phenomenon as best he could. Fortunately, Fleet-foot had listened to the portable radios of sportsmen on several occasions, and the Hardys were finally able to convince him that this was just another broadcast.

"How about the camp up there?" Joe asked. "Any signs that the gang might be coming back?"

Ted shook his head. "Not so far. But you know, there's one thing I can't figure out."

"What's that?"

"How come the fuel tank is completely empty? Robbie couldn't have figured out beforehand how much he'd need to fly here."

"No doubt the gang drained off the gas to keep anyone from flying the chopper away," Frank said. "Maybe there's a can of it hidden around here somewhere."

They searched the brush and examined the ground for any sign of digging, but all in vain.

"Well, what'll we do with the copter?" Joe asked finally. "Gas it up and try flying it to Juneau?"

"Not yet," Frank decided. "We've more sleuthing to do before we crack this mystery. If the gang found the whirlybird gone, they'd be on the alert. I vote we go upriver a bit and pick up the copter on our way back."

The others agreed to this plan. They returned to their canoes, unloaded the fuel cans which they had brought along, and quickly buried them. Then they embarked once more and continued their journey upriver.

As they paddled along, the four watched both shores like hawks, alert for the slightest sign of movement. But the wilderness lay steeped in brooding silence.

"Anyone have a suggestion about where to spend the night?" Joe finally asked as evening approached and dusk fell.

"How about the Hilton a little farther upstream?" Ted quipped.

"Suits me," Joe said and yawned.

"There's a good spot over there," Frank suggested. "It seems quite sheltered by the firs and the tall brush."

"Okay, we'll skip the Hilton and rough it," Joe said with a sigh.

They beached their canoes and made camp in the spot designated by Frank. On Fleetfoot's suggestion they did not light a campfire. After a cold supper of canned meat loaf and potato salad, they chose watches, then everyone prepared to turn in.

Some time later Frank, Joe, and Ted were quietly awakened by Fleetfoot. Except for a glimmer of moonlight through the evergreens, the river lay shrouded in darkness. A chilly night breeze was blowing down from the mountains.

"What's up, Fleetfoot?" Frank asked, instantly alert.

The Indian youth put his finger to his lips, then whispered, "Look over there—across the river."

The Hardys and Ted stared intently, their hearts pounding with excitement.

Lights flickered on the opposite shore!

CHAPTER XVI

An Eerie Sight

"The gang!" Ted gasped as the four stared at the moving lights across the river.

"Sure aren't fireflies!" Joe stated tersely. "How about it, Frank? Should we paddle over and see what they're up to?"

Frank pondered the situation with a worried frown. "If we try it, we may give ourselves away," he pointed out.

"We have rifles," Ted said.

Frank shook his head. "We want to avoid any shooting."

"Suppose we go back downriver where they can't spot us, and cross over?" Joe suggested. "Then we could sneak up on the other side and take them by surprise."

"It might work," Frank admitted.

"Unless they hear us hauling the canoe," Ted cautioned.

The boys conversed in low tones, discussing various plans. Fleetfoot finally settled the question by saying that he could paddle silently across the stream and scout the area without being detected. Knowing the young Indian's skill at canoeing and woodcraft, the boys agreed.

"Don't worry," Fleetfoot whispered. "When an Indian doesn't want to be seen, no one sees him. I'll be back soon!"

"Don't take any chances!" Frank told him.

The Hardys and Ted watched Fleetfoot creep through the underbrush. Keeping low, he reached the river's edge and slid his birchbark canoe noiselessly into the water. Then he slipped aboard and paddled out into midstream with smooth, silent strokes. In a few moments his ghostly figure melted from view in the darkness.

Tense moments passed. "He should be there by now," Frank whispered.

Suddenly the twinkling lights vanished as if turned off by a master switch. "Leapin' catfish!" Joe muttered. "They must have spotted Fleetfoot!"

"Don't jump to conclusions," Frank said calmly. "Perhaps the gang moved farther into the woods."

Joe and Ted alternately worried about whether Fleetfoot had been captured. Frank tried to allay their fears with a jest. "That would leave us up the creek without an Indian," he whispered.

Twenty minutes later, however, Frank began to feel a growing concern. The situation would certainly be more perilous than ever without Fleetfoot.

Suddenly, just as silently as he had left, the Indian reappeared at the side of his companions. Ted jumped with surprise and stared at him openmouthed.

"Boy! It's good to see you," Frank said. "What happened?"

"I saw four men," the Indian youth reported. "They were walking around with lights. Must have been searching for something."

"The lost rocket!" Joe exclaimed excitedly.

"Could be," Frank agreed. "Did you have a chance to hear what they were saying, Fleetfoot?"

The Indian shook his head. "Nothing. They were quiet, did not say a word. I think they must sleep in the daytime, and hunt only at night. That way they run into no danger from bears."

"You're probably right," Frank said. "Do they have a boat?"

"No boat," Fleetfoot replied. "I searched all along the shore."

"How about Robbie Robbins, the man who flies the whirlybird?" Joe asked. "Was he with them?"

Again Fleetfoot shook his head. "No. Robbins is young and tall. The men I saw were shorter and older."

"Then my dad couldn't be one of them, either," Ted put in quietly. "He's six-foot-two."

Excited by the events of the past hour, the boys were too wide awake to think of crawling back into their sleeping bags. For the next few minutes they discussed the mysterious goings on across the river.

Frank and Joe's conviction grew stronger that the ghostly search party might be looking for the rocket.

Finally Fleetfoot suggested that they break camp and push on upriver.

"Why?" Ted queried. "Do you think those men suspect we are over here?"

Fleetfoot shrugged. "I don't know. But even if they don't suspect it now, they might find out in the morning. And then we'd be in big trouble."

"Fleetfoot's right," Frank agreed. "It'll be safer to clear out now before they get wise to us." He stood silent for a minute, lost in thought. Then he said, "Come on! Let's head for those Indian grave houses. I have a hunch that's where we'll find the real key to this mystery!"

The others nodded. They put on their clothes and rolled up their sleeping bags, then they quietly piled their gear back in the canoes.

Ted had already heard the story of Jess Jenkins about the ancient Indian burial ground, but Fleetfoot had not been clued in yet. As the Hardys were getting ready to shove off, they passed the information on to their Indian friend.

"I've heard about that place," Fleetfoot said. "And I would certainly like to see it. I'll help you find it."

"You've already helped us a lot," Frank said gratefully, clapping the Indian youth on the back.

Once again Fleetfoot broke into his infectious grin. "You're right," he agreed proudly. "I sure am a *skookum* Indian."

The four now carefully covered all traces of their camp with leaves and brush. Suddenly Frank stood up straight. *"Sh!"* he warned.

Everyone froze and listened. A twig crackled behind Frank. Again. Then a small animal scurried by within ten feet.

"Wow!" Frank said. "That little bugger had me scared."

"I think it was a rabbit," Fleetfoot said.

Relieved, the boys launched their canoes and quickly climbed in. Soon they were paddling upriver through the darkness at a brisk clip.

Dawn found the canoeists many miles farther up the Kooniak. Halting for breakfast, they decided to refresh themselves first with a swim.

"Br-r-r! It's a regular ice bath!" Joe shuddered, after diving in.

"What's the matter? Can't you take it?" Frank joked, splattering him with a sheet of water.

Ted Sewell roared with laughter as the taunt developed into a water duel between the two Hardys. Fleetfoot, meanwhile, was plunging and darting like an otter, coming up every now and then to shake his long, black hair out of his eyes.

Shortly all of the boys were glad to hurry to dry land, where they toweled themselves to a brisk glow. After dressing, they ate a quick meal. Then they continued their journey.

An hour later Fleetfoot paused in his paddling and pointed to stone boundary markers on both banks of the stream. "Now we're in Canada," he told the others. "This is where the redcoats live."

"I guess you mean the Royal Canadian Mounted Police," Frank replied.

"That's right," Fleetfoot said.

The boys scanned the forest with eager interest. Though now in mountain country, they were again entering an area of dense wilderness. Both banks of the river were heavily timbered and overgrown with tangled green underbrush.

"Guess they don't need an immigration office at a wilderness place like this," Joe remarked with a smile.

Several miles east of the boundary markers, the boys saw a screaming horde of birds wheeling and circling over the right bank of the river. Gulls, terns, and grebes filled the air with their raucous cries.

"Hey, there's a blue heron!" Joe exclaimed as

the graceful creature rose above the treetops, flapping its wings.

"Why all the birds?" Frank wondered aloud.

"Must be a salmon spawning ground near," Ted conjectured.

"That's right," Fleetfoot said. "We'll see it very soon."

Presently they reached a point where the right bank of the river opened into a shallow cove. The backwater was swarming with salmon. Trout and walleyes, too, could be seen darting among the shallows.

"Wow! A fisherman's paradise!" Joe gasped. "Chet should be here!"

Every few moments one of the birds flocking overhead would swoop down and seize a fish in its beak.

"Birds eat young salmon," Fleetfoot explained. "Other fish eat salmon eggs, too."

"It's a wonder they survive," Frank remarked.

"They do, though—millions of them," said Ted. "Old Mother Nature sees to that."

"Mother Nature and the Fish and Wildlife Service!" Joe remarked wryly.

The river became more and more shallow as they continued upstream. Soon the canoes scraped the gravel bars that stretched from bank to bank.

"We'll make portage," Fleetfoot announced. "We're near the headwaters now."

"Wait a minute," Frank said slowly. He was

gazing at what seemed to be a dried-up creek bed, branching off to the west. "Joe, do you remember those two bends in the river we passed back a ways?"

"Sure. Why?"

"I believe this may be the spot shown on the map in the knapsack we found. That had a line branching off above two loops, just like that dry creek over there."

Joe's eyes widened with recognition. "You're right, Frank!" he said excitedly. "I'll bet this is the place! And maybe this is the creek Jess Jenkins was talking about that leads to the grave houses!"

"Let's find out," Frank replied.

After beaching the canoes, the boys unloaded their gear and covered everything carefully with stones and brush. Then they struck inland. Much of the creek bed was filled with reeds and waist-high grass. Heavy timber lined both banks.

A mile of walking brought them to a wide clearing which was becoming overgrown.

"Look! There they are!" Joe cried out.

The grave houses which Jess had described stood at scattered points about the area.

"This is it, all right," Frank declared, grinning. "The Indian burial ground!" Most of the small log structures were half-rotten and falling apart with age.

"Come on! Let's see what's inside them!" Joe

exclaimed. He ran to a rickety structure and stepped inside. "Oh!" he whispered. "Look at that!"

Frank, Ted, and Fleetfoot also stopped short and stared at the macabre spectacle. Gray, crumbling bones lay scattered beside a shallow open grave in the dirt floor. Fleetfoot stared at them fearfully. Then his eyes roved to a moldy wooden chest, which stood open nearby. It had apparently been lifted off the grave.

Joe glanced inside the chest and announced that it contained only a stone knife and a few small trinkets.

"Someone's been here before us," Frank muttered.

"Maybe this is one of the grave houses the prospectors looted back in Jess Jenkins' time," Joe suggested.

Frank shook his head. "I'm sure the grave hasn't been open that long."

One by one, they checked the other grave houses in the area. All had been rifled.

"Guess we're too late." Ted Sewell sighed.

"Maybe not," Joe said hopefully. "There's another one over there, among the trees. The door hasn't even been opened. Let's take a look."

The boys hurried over to inspect it, and found that the door gave easily to the first blow from a rifle butt. Inside, the dirt floor was untouched, and on it was a wooden chest, similar to the first, falling to pieces with age. A few streaks of blue and red paint still clung to its rotting surface.

"Hurry! Open it!" Ted blurted out.

Frank whipped out his knife. As he inserted the blade under the lid, the others watched breathlessly, wondering what they would find inside.

CHAPTER XVII

Buried Treasure

THE lid of the old chest creaked as Frank pried it open. Then Joe let out a whistle of awe.

"Jumpin' fishhooks! Will you look at that!"

The chest was heaped with jade necklaces, copper arm bands, delicate ivory figures carved from walrus tusks, and Oriental bowls fashioned of hammered metal. The boys' eyes bulged as Frank scooped out piece after piece and held it up for inspection.

"I'll bet this stuff's worth a fortune!" Ted gasped.

"Museums would probably pay plenty for it," Frank agreed.

"Look!" Joe seized one of the jade trinkets. "It's the same bird that was carved on the piece we found in the knapsack."

"I guess that clinches our deduction about the

treasure," Frank said, after carrying the piece out into the daylight so he could examine it more carefully. He added wryly, "We started out on this case as sleuths. But what with that dinosaur bone you spotted, Joe, and the ancient treasure, this seems to be turning into a scientific expedition!"

Fenton Hardy had often impressed on his two sons their responsibility for safeguarding any valuables which turned up during a case. Remembering this, Joe asked, "Frank, what are we going to do with this stuff? We can't just leave it here."

"I agree," Frank said. "If we do, it may be stolen before the authorities can pick it up."

"Why not take the chest with us?" Ted asked.

"We might be robbed," Joe objected. "There's too much danger of a brush with the gang."

"Besides," Frank pointed out, "I doubt if we have the right to carry such treasure out of British Columbia, even if we planned to turn it over to the Canadian authorities later."

After discussing the problem from every angle, the boys decided to bury the chest somewhere away from the grave houses. Then, at the earliest possible opportunity, they would notify the Canadian Mounted Police of their find.

Both Joe and Frank still were concerned about the code message they had intercepted in the singing wilderness. In case any of the gang might be spying on them, they insisted on combing the

trees and brush around the burial ground. Even
Fleetfoot's keen eyes, however, failed to detect
any trace of an enemy.

Satisfied that no one but themselves had seen
the treasure, Frank chose a tall cedar as a marker
for their cache.

"This should be easy to find again," he said.
"It's much taller than any of the other trees
around here."

"Okay," said Ted. "Let's get the chest."

Joe and Fleetfoot, meanwhile, had started back
to the canoes to fetch a camp spade and some oilskin. When they returned, the boys dug a hole
alongside the cedar, wrapped the chest in oilskin,
and after burying it, carefully replaced the earth.
This they covered with brush.

Before leaving, Ted suggested that they make
a final search of the area to be certain there was
no grave house which they might have overlooked.

"Good idea," Joe said eagerly. "We might find
more treasure."

Fanning out on both sides of the creek bed, the
boys forced their way through the heavy thickets
and peered among the dense groves of evergreens.
A low call from Joe brought the others hurrying
to his side. He was standing near a spot where the
forest thinned out into an area of swampy land.

"Look!" He pointed to the ground. In the soft
earth was a clear trail of footprints made by several men. Two sets of prints showed the same

circle-and-star heelmarks which the Hardys had seen before.

"The gang's been here all right," Frank said in a low voice.

Not far away was a trampled area which looked to the young sleuths as if it might have been the scene of a meeting. From this spot, most of the prints led back toward the river. One set of prints, however, headed off in a different direction.

"Let's follow this set," Frank suggested.

The boys proceeded cautiously, alert for any danger. Beyond the swamp area, the wilderness thickened again, with tangled underbrush pressing so close on every side that walking single file became necessary.

Taking the lead, Joe pushed on through the dense thickets. Behind him came Fleetfoot, then Ted and Frank.

Presently the forest thinned out somewhat, and Joe halted in surprise. Just ahead, partly screened by the trees, stood a cabin.

Apparently the noise of crashing through the underbrush had been heard by the occupants, for the cabin door suddenly opened and a man burst out, pointing a rifle in their direction.

He had on the striped trousers and boots of the Royal Canadian Mounted Police, but instead of the regulation brown tunic, he wore a checkered sports shirt.

"Halt!" the man shouted. "Don't move!"

"Halt!" the man shouted.

Just then a second man appeared in the cabin doorway. He was tall, bearded, and haggard looking. A chain was trailing from one of his ankles.

"Dad!" Ted gasped. "That other guy's no Mountie—he's a phony!"

In his excitement Ted would have rushed forward, in spite of the uniformed man's leveled rifle. Joe, however, grabbed his arm and held him back.

In a low whisper he called to Frank, who was still concealed from the view of the rifleman. "Sneak up behind him, Frank!"

Without another word, the older Hardy dropped on his hands and knees, worked his way back to denser cover, and made a circle of the cabin. He approached it from the rear as the gunman barked:

"Okay, you boy heroes! Move forward with your hands high!"

By this time Frank was peering around the corner of the cabin. Joe walked slowly, giving his brother time to act.

"Come on, there!" the man cried angrily. "I haven't got all day!"

Frank, meanwhile, tiptoed up behind him, hardly daring to breathe, lest he give himself away. Joe, Ted, and Fleetfoot looked on tensely as they approached, hands in the air.

Frank was now directly behind the phony Mountie!

"Ha-ha," the thug jeered. "The boss said I might get company. Now step— Ugh!"

The words were choked off as Frank crooked one arm around the man's windpipe, and snatched the rifle away, with the other. The man whirled and fought like a wildcat, but Frank wrestled him to the ground. Joe and Fleetfoot, rushing forward, quickly helped to subdue him.

"All right! On your feet!" Frank snapped, stepping back and covering the prisoner with his own rifle. Muttering, the man obeyed.

Ted, meanwhile, was having a joyful reunion with his father. "I can hardly believe it's you, son!" Mr. Sewell said huskily as he and Ted hugged each other. "This is too good to be true!"

"It *is* true, Dad! And we'll soon have that chain off!"

Frank ordered the impostor to surrender the key to Joe, who quickly unlocked the shackle from around Mr. Sewell's ankle. The wildlife expert then told his story. He had discovered the same singing wilderness which the boys had come across the previous day.

"I couldn't figure out who was broadcasting," Mr. Sewell related, "but I decided to report the matter to Juneau. Before I could do so, several men jumped me from behind. They brought me upriver in a boat, and then marched me inland to this cabin. I've been chained up here ever since."

Frank wanted to ask if Mr. Sewell had heard the gang mention anything about the lost rocket, but decided against it. "No sense letting our prisoner in on what we know," he thought. Turning to Fleetfoot, he directed, "Take this fellow away from the cabin and keep him covered, will you?" The Indian nodded, borrowed Ted's rifle, and herded the captive out of earshot.

Then Frank turned back to Mr. Sewell. "We believe this gang may be led by foreigners, but that phony Mountie speaks like an American. Any idea who he is?"

Mr. Sewell shook his head. "I don't even know his name. The other men called him 'Watchdog.' However, from his accent, I'd say he comes from Chicago!"

The Hardys gave Mr. Sewell a quick summary of the whole case to date, including their finding of the Indian treasure at the burial ground. The woodsman was astounded, but could offer no solution to the mystery.

"The men who captured me were careful not to say anything which might give me a clue," he explained. "However, I once overheard them mention the word 'totem.' "

"Meaning what, do you suppose?" Joe asked. "A totem pole?"

"Probably so. Perhaps they're using one as a landmark."

"It may mark the spot where they've cached

the loot from the Indian grave houses," Frank conjectured.

"It's possible," Joe agreed.

"We'd better get out of here before someone comes back and sees us," Ted urged. "Dad, do you think you'll be able to walk for a while?"

Mr. Sewell nodded. "I have no choice. Rusty muscles or not. But listen, let's take some food. There's canned meat in the cabin, also bread and fruit."

Ted's father had been fed little more than scraps during his captivity, and was obviously in need of nourishment. The boys, too, were growing very hungry and took whatever they could stuff into their pockets.

Then they started back toward the river with their prisoner. Once during the trek Watchdog tried to escape, but the boys quickly forced him back on the trail.

Mr. Sewell began to ache badly after a while. Even though he tried not to show it, Ted knew his father was weak and barely able to make it.

"Let's stop over there and eat," he suggested. "It will give Dad a chance to recuperate a little." He pointed to a secluded spot on the side of a rock.

They sat down, covered from view by shrubs and trees, and quickly distributed the food.

Ted produced a can opener. "I found this in one of the cabinets," he said.

"Sure comes in handy," Frank said with a grin, and opened a can of ham.

"This is the best meal I ever had," Mr. Sewell said. "I'm starting to feel better already."

Soon they were finished and on their way again. Suddenly a shrill birdcall shattered the silence of the forest.

"Hey! What was that?" Joe exclaimed as he and the others turned around, scanning the branches of the nearby trees.

Mr. Sewell was particularly puzzled. "I've never heard a birdcall like that!" he declared. "I wonder—"

His words broke off at a shout of dismay by Frank. "The prisoner! He's gone!"

CHAPTER XVIII

The Totem's Secret

THE boys glanced about in consternation. Watchdog had vanished as suddenly as the strange birdcall had stopped!

Frank was now red-faced with anger. "After him!" he exclaimed.

"But which direction did he take?" Ted asked. "He was so quiet we don't know where he is. And it's easy to hide here in the woods."

"We'll split up! Let's go!"

Frank and Fleetfoot disappeared into the bushes on the right, while Joe and Ted searched the area on the left side. Discouraged after their ten-minute futile search, the four boys joined Ted's father who had waited on the trail.

"I just remembered that Watchdog is a ventriloquist," he told them. "He used to practice at the cabin to pass away the time. He projected that birdcall, and while we were gawking around, he sneaked off!"

Suddenly Fleetfoot pointed. "There are his footprints. I'll find him now!"

The youth started off at a quick lope, Frank and Joe following at his heels. Ted and his father hurried along behind them. The searchers moved quietly, every sense alert.

Soon the Indian boy stopped and raised his right hand. The searchers came to a halt. Fleetfoot beckoned them forward and pointed to a massive rock formation which loomed up on one side of a creek bed. At the foot of it was a black, gaping hole, obviously the entrance to a cave.

"How are we going to flush him?" Ted wanted to know.

Frank was worried that the cave might have an exit as well. "I'll scout around back of those rocks to see if there's a way out."

He had gone only three feet when a hoarse cry emitted from the opening in the rocks!

The weird cry issued forth again. Frank and Joe screwed up their courage and advanced closer to the black hole.

All at once the head and shoulders of a man appeared. Crawling on all fours, he scrambled out of the cave like a beaten animal.

"Watchdog!" Frank yelled.

The fugitive sprang to his feet and rushed forward in headlong flight. As Frank and Joe converged upon him, Watchdog tripped on a root and fell to the ground with a thud.

"Got you!" Frank cried. He grasped Watch-dog's arms and held them behind his back.

Then, just as suddenly, Frank sprang off his prisoner. "Whew!" he exclaimed, sniffing. "Skunk!"

In spite of the gravity of the situation, every-one except the prisoner, who lay half stunned and gasping for breath, burst out laughing.

"There comes our friend!" Fleetfoot pointed to the cave entrance. A small black animal with a white streak down his back poked his nose out into the underbrush.

"Mr. Polecat deserves a medal!" Joe said, dou-bling over with mirth.

"But what about Watchdog?" Ted grinned. "How can we travel with a smell like that?"

"A bath will help," Frank said. He and Joe led Watchdog to a nearby creek.

"Jump in," Frank ordered, unable to suppress a wry smile. "Clothes and all."

Watchdog obliged. He dived into the water and splashed about, at the same time emitting uncom-plimentary remarks both about the skunk and his captors.

"I'll get even for this." Watchdog glowered as he stepped from the creek and wrung the water from his clothes.

Mr. Sewell could not suppress a grin. "You certainly picked the wrong hiding place!"

Frank then turned to their prisoner. "Just to

see that you don't try any tricks, we'll keep you close to us!"

"Hey, not too close," Joe begged as Frank pulled off his belt and tied Watchdog's hands securely behind him.

"Now listen," Frank told Watchdog sternly, "we'll travel single file. You stay five paces behind me. Joe, you keep about the same distance behind this guy."

Anxious not to lose any more time, the group proceeded to the river at a brisk pace. Here the canoes were uncovered and reloaded. Frank retrieved his belt while Joe rebound the prisoner's hands with rope. Then he was placed in the bottom of one of the canoes and covered with a piece of tarpaulin, in case other members of his gang should appear along the way.

"We ought to report what's happened," Joe said. "Do you think we can raise Juneau on the radio?"

Frank set to work immediately, but after hoisting the aerial, he could get only static over his headset.

"Terrific interference," he told Joe. "Sounds as if there's some electrical device here in the woods."

"Like what?" Ted asked.

"Perhaps someone else has a powerful radio," Mr. Sewell put in.

Joe winked at his brother. "Maybe a dentist has an office nearby," he said.

Frank gave his brother a thump on the arm. "Stow the corny jokes, Joe!"

The lighthearted attitude of the Hardys continued after they had launched their canoe into the stream. With Ted and his father paddling alongside them, Frank and Joe fairly shot along with the current.

"Boy, this is what I call fun!" Joe exulted as they sped through the foaming rapids.

They crossed the boundary line at a fast clip and mile after mile went by under the swift stroke of their paddles. At seven o'clock they beached their canoes long enough to eat supper.

"Frank," Joe said, "you can hand-feed Skunkie Boy over there. I wouldn't advise untying him again."

"I caught him, so I guess I'm stuck with him." Frank grinned and moved over to where the prisoner lay in the canoe.

"Sit up," Frank said. "I'll feed you your beans. Watch your manners."

Watchdog chewed glumly as he ate his supper.

"If you want room service during the night," Frank jested, "push the button."

The sinister outline of Devil's Paw looming in the distance, however, brought the boys back to awareness of their grim situation.

"Are we going to camp here tonight?" Ted queried.

After a hasty conference, both the Hardys and Mr. Sewell decided against such a move.

"We ought to get our prisoner back to Juneau as soon as possible," the woodsman suggested.

Frank and Joe agreed. "Suppose you and Ted take him along," Frank said.

"And leave you here?"

"The three of us will be safe enough," he assured the Sewells.

Joe declared that they should at least stop at the enemy's camp long enough to see whether Robbie had returned to the helicopter.

"All right," Mr. Sewell acceded. "Ted and I will go on and report everything that has happened, but be careful."

It was still daylight by the time the adventurers re-embarked and reached the point on the west bank of the river near the trail which led to the camp at Devil's Paw. Here the Hardys made another attempt to get in touch with Juneau by radio. This time the static was even louder.

"Boy! This is a real mystery!" Joe removed his headphones. "We're getting interference from something mighty powerful."

The Sewells stopped along the riverbank to say good-by, then paddled out of sight along the foaming river. After they had gone, Frank, Joe, and Fleetfoot turned their attention to the job

of caching the two remaining canoes and their
supplies.

Joe suggested that they also check on the fuel
cans which they had hidden earlier. They found
them still in place and Fleetfoot reported no footprints were in evidence nearby.

Once again the three companions followed the
beaten trail up the mountainside to the camp.
Dodging behind the trees and peering from be-
neath the bushes, they silently approached the
area. Nobody was in sight.

Suddenly Joe clutched his brother's arm. "Look
over there," he said.

"What do you know about that? Robbie's
sweater!"

The three boys stepped forward to examine it.
It was a blue garment with red trim. The way it
lay on the ground, however, made Frank suspect
that it had not been dropped accidentally.

"Look!" he said, and indicated the left arm of
the sweater. "See how the sleeve is pointing, Joe."

"That was done on purpose!" Joe exclaimed.

"Of course. Robbie put this here to give us
directions."

Fleetfoot spoke up approvingly. "Robbie is like
a good Indian. He gave a sign."

The sweater arm pointed southwest over an
area of rock and shale. The ground was too hard
to reveal any footprints.

Frank and Joe left the sweater untouched as

a safety precaution, in case they lost their way and wanted to find the trail again. Then they set off with Fleetfoot. Gradually the ground sloped away to a heavily wooded valley. Just before the edge of the timber, Fleetfoot's keen eyes noted several sets of footprints leading in the direction they were going.

"We are on the right track," he said.

With extreme caution, the three boys pushed their way among the pines and underbrush. The forest was wrapped in a brooding silence. The setting sun shone blood red over the hills.

The Hardys and Fleetfoot continued on through the towering trees. Frank was the first to step out into a small clearing. Silently he beckoned to the others.

"What's the matter?" asked Joe.

Frank pointed. "There, next to that leaning pine tree."

Joe shielded his eyes with his hands to keep out the sun's glare.

"By golly, Frank, that's a thunderbird!"

The figure stood out above the tall grass, and when Fleetfoot saw it, he said, "That's the top of a totem pole."

Advancing cautiously, the boys came upon a ten-foot post, with angry-looking faces of salmon, bears, and sea otters with bared fangs.

At the top of the totem, a thunderbird leered down at them with outspread wings. Though badly weather-beaten, the pole still showed traces of red, yellow, and blue paint.

"Could the pole be a landmark?" Joe asked.

"I'm sure it's more than that," Frank reasoned, "because the footprints led directly to it. This thunderbird totem must be of some special importance."

The Indian boy's hands were moving over the carved images. He turned to grin at his two companions. "Sometime totem pole hide important messages." Fleetfoot next felt around the indented mouth of the salmon.

"No message here," he said, disappointed.

Joe glanced up. "What about the thunderbird? Could that have a message in it?"

Fleetfoot shrugged. Whereupon Joe said, "Come on, Frank, give me a boost. I'll take a look for myself."

Frank cupped his hands together waist-high, and Joe placed his right foot in the hand stirrup.

"Up you go!" Frank gave Joe a strong boost.

Joe deftly put a foot on either of his brother's shoulders. He was now high enough to reach the thunderbird.

"Look in the beak," Fleetfoot said.

"False alarm," Joe reported. "The bird doesn't have a message and— Hey! Watch it, Frank. Don't wriggle like that!"

Frank had moved slightly to slap at a mosquito, and in doing so had thrown Joe off balance. He pitched to one side, brushing against the right wing of the thunderbird. It fell off.

"Look out below!" Joe cried. He hit the ground with a thud. The wing just missed his head.

"You hurt?" Fleetfoot asked.

"I'm all right," Joe said, getting up and rubbing his thigh. "But look at the totem pole. I guess I ruined it."

The three boys glanced up to the place where the wing had been ripped off the towering figure.

Fleetfoot whistled. "That was meant to come off! See? There's a hole in the totem pole."

"Wow!" Joe exclaimed. "Let's investigate!"

This time Frank was hoisted to the shoulders of Joe and the Indian, who stood side by side. Tense with excitement, he reached up into the opening.

"Hey, fellows!" he cried out. "Something's in here!"

CHAPTER XIX

Enmeshed

JOE and Fleetfoot stared upward as Frank withdrew his hand from the opening in the totem pole.

"What did you find?" Joe called.

"A canvas sack. And is it heavy!"

When Frank had pulled the large sack free of the hole, he leaped nimbly to the ground with it. Then, quickly unloosening the drawstring, he dumped the contents onto the ground.

"Look at that!" Joe cried out. "More treasure!"

"From grave houses!" Fleetfoot declared instantly. He picked up several of the ornaments and examined them curiously.

Frank spoke up. "Joe, this stuff must be priceless! I'll bet there's nothing like it, even in the Alaska Historical Museum!"

Joe reflected for a moment. "Do you suppose

Robbie pointed the sweater sleeve this way to lead us to the thunderbird's cache?"

"I don't think so," Frank said. "He was probably interested only in where he was going—or being taken."

"Treasure or no," Joe said, "Robbie's safety is more important. But, meanwhile, what'll we do with this?"

"Same thing we did before," Fleetfoot said. "We'll bury it, just like the other stuff. But first we must put back the thunderbird's wing."

Standing on Frank's shoulder, Joe quickly replaced the wing, covering the opening. Fleetfoot had found a cleft between two rocks which he thought might be a good hiding place for the treasure. The boys laid the canvas sack in the depression, and covered it with a layer of brush, then a rotted tree limb which lay nearby.

After the artifacts were concealed, they trekked on, following the same direction as before. They scanned the ground and their surroundings for any other clue Robbie might have left, but found nothing.

All of a sudden, about ten minutes later, Frank stopped short.

"Fleetfoot, Joe! Look here!" He pointed to a sapling. A branch, close to the ground, was freshly broken.

"A marker!" Fleetfoot said, examining it closely.

"You think Robbie did that to indicate a change in the direction?" Joe asked.

"Looks that way," Frank said. "It points over there, to the right."

"Let's follow it," Fleetfoot said. "You see the sap still oozing from the branch? It was only broken a little while ago, and I'm sure Robbie did it. He was on his toes, all right."

"But we'd better be quiet," Frank warned.

The boys alternated in taking the lead through the dense underbrush. As they topped a low rise of ground, Fleetfoot motioned the Hardys to stop and listen. They put their ears to the ground.

"Someone's walking up ahead," Frank whispered.

"Yes. Many feet," the Indian said. "We must be careful."

Creeping forward on hands and knees, the boys inched to the top of the knoll. There, completely hidden by foliage, they looked down into a small ravine. Below them was a group of men going through mysterious motions!

"One, two, four—six of them," Joe counted to himself.

In their hands all of the men held long poles which they were moving back and forth over the ground and bushes.

Frank leaned close to his brother. "Detecting equipment!" he exclaimed in a whisper.

"No wonder our radio's been full of static!"

Joe whispered back. "These birds must have been pretty close to us all the time."

Frank touched Fleetfoot on the shoulder and motioned for him to withdraw. The three boys ducked below the brow of the hill. In an undertone Frank quickly explained the situation to Fleetfoot.

"They're looking for the rocket, all right," he said, "and it's not dark yet. They must be getting desperate to find it."

"But where's Robbie?" Joe whispered. "You don't suppose they've—?"

"I don't think they'd harm him," Frank said. "Robbie is their ace in the hole—they might need him in case they have to escape by helicopter."

"We'd better take a closer look," Joe suggested.

"Follow me," Fleetfoot said.

Depending on their Indian friend's acute sense of direction, the boys hunched low and crept after him in a circuitous route which led down to one end of the ravine. Then darting from tree to tree in the deepening evening shadows, the three approached nearer to the six men.

Suddenly one of them straightened up and leaned on his detector. "What a wild-goose chase!"

"Yeah," another man said. "It doesn't make sense. What could they drop out of an airplane that was so valuable?"

"Oh, them foreigners don't give you any straight answers," a third man spoke up. "They're pretty clever, and after all, they're paying us enough."

"Not enough to keep this poor guy tied up," another of the gang members called.

A voice sounded from behind a large tree ten yards ahead of the Hardys. "Let me go, will you, fellows? Maybe I can help you out of the mess you're in."

"Robbie!" Frank whispered.

"You ain't got enough money to buy us," one of the men called back. "After all, we've got to make a living!"

Fleetfoot, who had pressed close to the Hardys, whispered, "These men are no good. Loafers. I have seen them hanging around the dock at Ketchikan."

Frank nodded. "I don't think we can talk them into letting Robbie go. We've got to get him out of here ourselves."

"But how?" Joe asked.

"Let's wait a while and see what happens."

Fortunately, the six searchers moved farther away from the spot where the captive pilot was sitting. After ten minutes Frank motioned to his companions. "Let's get over to Robbie, but easy! If we scare him, he might yell!"

The three boys inched along the ground, using

every blade of tall grass as cover until they were behind the tree from which Robbie's voice had come.

"Robbie! *Robbie!*" Frank whispered hoarsely.

"Wh—?"

"Sh!"

But Robbie's startled outcry had alerted one of his captors. He straightened up and turned in their direction.

"What'd you say, skipper?"

"Why don't you let me go?" Robbie called back promptly. "I might have more money than you think. We can talk about it."

"Forget it!" The man shrugged and resumed his search.

In a hushed voice, Robbie said, "Frank, Joe, is that you?"

"Yes," Frank whispered. "Be quiet. We're trying to get you out of here."

Frank peered around the side of the tree. Robbie's hands were tied behind his back and his ankles were bound with leather thongs.

"Lie down," Frank said, "and stretch out as if you're taking a nap."

Robbie did as he was instructed, holding his wrists and ankles close to the side of the tree. In the dim light the hands of Frank and Joe were barely visible as they reached around to cut the bonds of the helicopter pilot.

Robbie moved his arms and legs slowly so as to

regain circulation. This accomplished he slithered around the tree, unnoticed by the gang. Then, with the tree as a shield, he stood up. Fleetfoot motioned the three to follow and they set off at a rapid pace through the underbrush.

At first Robbie had difficulty keeping up with the boys because of cramps in his legs. These, however, were soon worked out and he was able to jog swiftly along beside his rescuers.

They were breathing hard as they hurried through the tangled woods. Part of Robbie's story of what had happened came out when the group stopped for a short rest.

"Those men probably haven't discovered you're missing yet," Joe said. "All is quiet." Then he added, "Who are those fellows, Robbie?"

"Renegades from down the coast somewhere. They're working for those foreigners. Oh, I'd like to get my hands on that guy who kidnapped me!"

"What was his name?" asked Frank.

"Remus—or something like that."

"Remo Stransky!" Frank exclaimed.

"How did he get away with it?" Joe asked the pilot.

"Pushed a gun in my back just as I was about to take off for the glacier to pick up you boys."

"But what about the package dropped to us by the airplane?" Joe asked, perplexed.

"Remo bragged that a friend would do that,"

Robbie told them, "just to throw you off the trail."

"Did you write the note?"

"Yes. I was forced to."

Fleetfoot spoke up. "Do you know what these men are looking for?"

"No, not exactly. Something very important."

Robbie told them his foreign captors had stated that one of their country's airplanes had dropped valuable cargo by mistake. The United States government allegedly would not cooperate in helping them find it. "So," concluded Robbie, "they decided to take matters into their own hands."

"What a phony story" Joe declared. "They're looking for that rocket."

Just then shouts of angry men echoed through the darkening woods.

"They've found out you've escaped!" said Frank. "Come on Let's go!"

Like a slender brown ghost, Fleetfoot led them racing through the woodlands along a trail barely perceptible in the gloom. Five minutes later the cries of their pursuers were lost in the distance.

"We've shaken them," Joe said.

"Don't be too sure," Frank cautioned. He turned to Robbie. "Do they have a radio?"

"Yes. A strong transceiver."

"Then they'll report this to Stransky," Frank said. "We've got to be extra careful."

The four jogged along at an easier pace and the helicopter pilot told more of his story. The foreign gang, hunting for the valuable cargo in the woodlands, had come upon the Indian grave houses and rifled them.

Robbie related that he did manage to drop his sweater and break the tree branch to mark the trail without his captors noticing. "They got careless about watching me," he went on. "Too busy looking for a spot to stash the loot."

Frank interrupted. "They found a place—in the thunderbird totem."

Robbie was amazed. "How'd you find it?"

The Hardys gave him a brief account of Joe's accidental discovery. The gang, Robbie said, had also come upon the hiding place by chance. "And that salmon-poaching business," he added, "was just a cover-up for this giant search."

The pilot was delighted to hear that the boys had brought cans of aviation fuel and cached them near the riverbank.

It was decided that they would leave their canoes, as well as the treasure, hidden, and take off with Robbie in the helicopter.

"Now that we know where these fellows are," Frank said, "a flying police detail can help us round them up."

Skirting Devil's Paw at a safe distance, the four made their way down the steep slope toward Robbie's helicopter. The moon had come up, and cast a luminous glow on the sides of the craft.

"Well, here she is safe and sound," Robbie said, putting his foot on a rung at the side of the chopper. He was just about to climb into the cabin when a sudden swishing sound filled the air. Frank, Joe, and Fleetfoot, poised behind the pilot, whirled about.

"Look out, Frank!" Joe called as he saw the dim figures of five men leap suddenly out from the shadow of a boulder.

At the same time a large fishnet fell over the heads and shoulders of Frank and the Indian boy!

CHAPTER XX

Aerial Roundup

WITH cries and whoops the five attackers rushed upon the boys. Frank and Fleetfoot, entangled in the net, could offer little assistance as the assailants fought to subdue Joe and Robbie.

In five minutes all four lay exhausted on the ground. Their hands had been tied behind them by the gloating victors.

As one of the gang examined the bonds, he rasped in English, "Nice work with the net, Igor. We got 'em all. Herd 'em together and tie the seine around the bunch. We have our fish."

"Remo Stransky!" Joe lunged out at him, but in vain. Stransky laughed in the youth's face.

"Save your strength!" he taunted. "This seine is made of your American nylon and is quite unbreakable." Stransky's lips curled gloatingly. "You Hardys and your two foolish friends here will never leave this forest alive."

"Don't be too sure of that!" Frank retorted. "Besides, whatever happens to us, Stransky, you and your gang will be caught."

The ringleader threw back his head and laughed harshly. "I'll say this much for you Hardys, you never give up. You and your buddies have found out a great deal, too much in fact, but my countrymen and I will not be cheated of success!"

The Hardys, Robbie, and Fleetfoot were searched and their hunting knives taken away.

"We'll relieve you of these," Stransky said with a sneer, "so you can't cut your way to freedom." Then he spoke into a small walkie-talkie which one of his henchmen handed to him.

"Okay, my American allies," he said. "We have snared the Hardys and the others. You will get a bonus for this." Then he added, "Keep on looking there until I instruct you further."

Stransky turned to his captives. "Come now," he said, "we have no time to waste."

To his henchmen, Stransky gave crisp orders. Two of them immediately jerked the prisoners around and headed them toward the trail leading up to the Devil's Paw camp. Straining and sweating, the captives were half dragged, half shoved along the rocky trail. It was dark by the time they reached the camp.

Stransky spoke again into the walkie-talkie. "Assemble at camp, men!"

Robbie and the boys were glad to have a chance

to lie down. All were aching, parched, and hungry.

"This is outrageous!" Robbie muttered.

"Calm yourself," Stransky called out with a hoarse laugh. Then he directed one of his men, "Guard them closely, so they don't escape while we prepare supper."

The guard, who spoke English, as well as Stransky's native tongue, stretched down on the ground beside the prisoners. He taunted the Hardys. "I understand you found the boss's knapsack. A lot of good it did you!"

"How did you know that?" Frank asked.

"One of our spies in Juneau told us." The guard laughed raucously. "Fish! Salmon in the seine! Ha-ha!"

"You'll laugh out of the other side of your mouth," Joe muttered. "Just wait."

"Quiet!"

"What do you intend to do with us?" Frank asked.

"What usually happens to unwanted fish?" the man sneered. "You throw them into the ocean."

His compatriots, meanwhile, had started a roaring campfire. The light flickered over the faces of the four prisoners who reclined glumly in the shadow of some tall bushes.

About twenty minutes later the sound of many footsteps crashing through the woods brought the Hardys alert.

"Joe! Maybe it's a rescue party!" Frank said.

But the boys were doomed to disappointment, for into the circle of firelight stepped the gang's American henchmen carrying mine detectors.

"So you caught 'em, eh?" said one.

"Yeah," another said with a chuckle. "I hear those Hardys are just a couple of amateur detectives."

"Boy, I wish Dad were here now," Joe thought, furious. "We'd show 'em who are amateurs."

To add to the misery of the trapped quartet, their captors brought a steaming tin of stew to the guard. The aroma wafted to their nostrils, causing their mouths to water. But they remained silent, determined to ask no favors.

Soon the group around the campfire were eating and joking loudly.

"Now that the Hardys and their friends are tied up," Stransky said, "we can go ahead in our search without any more trouble."

"What about the reinforcements, boss?"

"They're on the way," Stransky replied. "They'll skip past Prito and his fat friend tonight. With ten more fellows helping, you should find that—er—lost cargo in no time."

Frank and Joe exchanged glances of alarm. If they could only warn Chet and Tony of the impending peril! "It looks as if it's curtains for all of us!" Joe whispered glumly.

After the meal, the captives and their guard

were swallowed up in the shadows. Frank had started to doze when suddenly he was snapped to consciousness by the sound of a groan.

Startled, the Hardys saw to their astonishment that it was their guard who had uttered the sound!

Suddenly a voice close to them whispered, "How're you fellows? All right?"

"*Chet!*" Frank gasped. "Are you alone?"

"No, I'm here too," came another voice.

"Tony!" Joe said in muffled but joyful tones.

"Well, we took care of that guy for a while," said Chet. "I jumped on his middle, then Tony socked him."

"Sure good to see you!" Fleetfoot said.

"You bet!" Robbie spoke up. "Hope you brought a sharp knife."

"Right here. I'll have you out in a jiffy." Tony glanced quickly at the men about the campfire. Some were now asleep, others were lolling about. Desultory chatter muffled the sound of Tony's knife as it cut through the strands of the seine.

"There," he said finally. "You're free. Let's get out of here."

"Where to?" asked Chet.

"Robbie's copter," replied Frank. "I think we can make it this time."

Tony held out a small compass attached to his belt. The luminous face gave the group their bearings. Then, with Fleetfoot in the lead, the six stealthily crept away.

Keeping tensely on the alert for signs of pursuit, they proceeded for some time in dead silence. Finally, feeling they were safely out of earshot, Joe asked Chet and Tony, "How'd you find us, fellows?"

"Easy," Tony said. "We spotted that campfire a mile away."

As the boys walked on, Chet told Frank and Joe they had become worried about their friends' long absence.

"Tony got half a dozen guards as replacements to take charge at the island," he added, "so we could come to look for you."

Frank slapped the stout boy affectionately on the shoulder. Chet's loyalty was unswerving.

Once Fleetfoot had found the slope leading to the helicopter, the party cautiously traversed the rocky terrain. Frank and Joe, with the aid of Tony and Chet, carried the cans of gasoline from their hiding place. Upon reaching the helicopter, they fueled it. Robbie, meanwhile, checked the instrument panel, as Fleetfoot looked on with awe.

"Do I get my whirlybird ride now?"

"Right!" Joe said. "You certainly deserve it!"

Preparations for the flight went on under mounting tension. Every few moments Frank or Joe glanced up at the rocky cliff to see whether or not Stransky's men were pursuing them.

Finally Robbie announced, "Okay, we're set to go, but I've got bad news."

"What's that?" Joe said.

"I can't take all of you out in one trip. Two must be left behind."

"I'll stay," Joe volunteered.

"Me too," Chet offered without hesitation.

Frank protested at first, saying he wanted to stay with his brother. But Joe insisted that Frank go back to give details of their adventure to the authorities in Juneau.

With snappy salutes, Chet and Joe bade their companions farewell. The door of the helicopter closed. With a whining sound the rotors turned, slowly at first, then whirred into full action.

Suddenly, above the noise of the rotors, Joe and Chet heard a volley of rifleshots from the cliff.

"Run for cover!" Joe cried out.

The two boys darted behind a boulder. "Will the copter get off in time?" Joe wondered, his heart pounding. The lives of Frank and the three others aboard were at stake! Breathlessly Joe and Chet watched as the helicopter rose, gained sufficient altitude, and took forward flight. Seconds later the chopper blinked its running lights.

"Thank goodness!" Joe exclaimed. "They're safe!"

The helicopter pilot had worked feverishly to get out of range of the snipers. The first indication of enemy fire had been a bullet ripping through the fuselage close to Frank's head.

Now beyond reach of the guns, Frank, Tony,

and Robbie conferred. "Better contact Juneau pronto," Frank said.

"Right!" Robbie flicked on the radio.

It took only a few minutes to relay the urgent summons. The operator at the seaplane base promised to alert the authorities, not only in the state of Alaska, but also in British Columbia.

"Now what?" Tony asked.

"We'll stand by," Frank replied. "Shouldn't take long."

In less than an hour, aircraft of both the United States and Canadian forces came streaking low over the woods. Robbie had pinpointed their location.

As if by magic, the darkness suddenly turned to daylight. Powerful magnesium flares attached to parachutes illuminated the entire area. This was followed by more billowing chutes—paratroops! They ringed the area and their walkie-talkie reports could be heard plainly over the radio of the hovering copter.

The action was swift and conclusive. The fleeing enemy, hampered by swampy ground and the dark night, were hunted down. In a few hours the gang had been rounded up.

"Good show. Better than a cowboy movie!" Fleetfoot exclaimed.

The others laughed. Then Frank urged, "Let's get an Army helicopter to go down with us and pick up Joe and Chet."

Robbie radioed the request and received an affirmative reply.

"We'll stand by to follow you in," came the Army pilot's voice.

Robbie set his craft down at the place where they had left the two boys. Magnesium flares still drifting down from the sky illuminated the area. Finally Chet and Joe dashed out from between two large boulders. They reached the helicopter as the Army craft came in alongside.

"Frank" Joe called excitedly as his brother jumped down from the chopper. "We found it! We found it!"

"What?" Frank asked, running up.

"The rocket! It made a crater just beyond the place where we were hiding."

Joe and Chet led the others to the spot. Only part of the metal hull could be seen protruding from the sandy spot where the rocket had landed.

"This is it all right!" Robbie declared.

Moments later a colonel from the Air Force joined the boys. When told about the find, he quickly swore them all to secrecy.

"You've done your country a tremendous service," he praised the Hardys and their friends, then hastened off to radio a coded report to Washington.

A little later Robbie's group took off in his helicopter, while Joe and Chet boarded the Army chopper for the ride back to Juneau.

"Wow, what excitement!" Joe exclaimed as he sat down.

At the moment he had no way of knowing that more excitement was to come the Hardys' way very soon. In their next adventure, *The Mystery of the Chinese Junk,* the two young sleuths are plunged into danger when they try to find the solution to a baffling puzzle.

The Hardys and the others rendezvoused at the air base in Juneau. There they learned that Remo's reinforcements had been captured at the mouth of the Kooniak. Frank and Joe quickly put through a radio message to their father in Bayport and took turns telling of their adventures.

"I'm mighty proud of you," Fenton Hardy said, after hearing the full story. "Are you going back for the buried treasure?"

"Tomorrow, Dad."

Just then Tony Prito brought in more news, which was relayed by Frank to Bayport. The prisoner, nicknamed Watchdog, had finally confessed to police that his real name was Shad Yawke. He had been hired by the Stranskys to terrorize the stream guard on duty in the Kooniak. He had also hired the salmon poachers to mislead the Hardys, in case they should guess the foreign ring's true purpose—that of finding the rocket.

Yawke confirmed Frank's suspicion about the star-heel imprint which the boys had found in so many places. It was the trademark of a foreign manufacturer whose shoes were worn by the alien gang.

"A stupid oversight by the Stranskys," Joe commented.

The captured henchman admitted, too, the hurling of the fire bomb and the looting of the Indian grave houses by the gang. Further interrogation revealed that he knew about the ancient Indian paddle. One of the gang had taken the paddle and subsequently lost it when spying on Tony Prito.

Mr. Hardy supplied his sons with additional information about Romo Stransky's activities.

"When Romo learned from his twin that Tony was sending for you boys," Mr. Hardy related. "he tried to prevent you from leaving Bayport."

"And was he the truck driver who forced us off the road?"

"Yes."

"Well, I guess that clears up the mystery, Dad. We'll be home soon." Frank said good-by and hung up.

At that moment Chet walked into the radio room, his face beaming. "There's one thing I didn't tell you fellows about."

"What's that? Did you dig up some more crooks, Chet?" Frank asked with a twinkle.

"No," the boy said. "I caught a salmon, a twenty-pound beaut. We're going to have a real feast tonight. Fleetfoot will cook it Indian style."

Frank and Joe chuckled. "Here's one time I'm with you," Joe said, pumping the stout boy's hand. "I'm hungry."

"Me, too!" Frank agreed heartily.

"Call the fellows together." Joe grinned. "This will be one salmon the Alaskan bears won't get!"